ONE DOWN

It was close. Charley Crow moved like a silent shadow in the night, and he struck like lightning. His knife went straight for Skye Fargo's heart—and came damn close to hitting home.

Fargo did the only thing he could do. He let go of his useless Colt and grabbed the breed's knife arm with both hands, twisted sharply, shifted, and speared the killer's own knife up into Charley Crow's gut.

Fargo talked fast, while Crow could still speak. "Why does Morgan want me dead? Why were all those others killed?"

Charley Crow's mouth moved as if to speak, but instead spit, aimed at Fargo's face, came flying out. It fell short, onto the tip of Fargo's boot.

"With my dying breath I curse you, white-eye! I hope the others kill you! I hope they make you suffer!" He would have gone on had the end not dawned. His legs buckled, and he pitched onto his chest and was still.

Skye Fargo spoke his epitaph. "Good riddance, bastard."

The Trailsman was lucky to be alive. But how long would that luck hold . . . ?

**Be sure to read the other
books in the exciting Trailsman series
about the Old West!**

THE TRAILSMAN

166

COLORADO CARNAGE

by

Jon Sharpe

A SIGNET BOOK

SIGNET
Published by the Penguin Group
Penguin Books USA Inc., 375 Hudson Street,
New York, New York 10014, U.S.A.
Penguin Books Ltd, 27 Wrights Lane,
London W8 5TZ, England
Penguin Books Australia Ltd, Ringwood,
Victoria, Australia
Penguin Books Canada Ltd, 10 Alcorn Avenue,
Toronto, Ontario, Canada M4V 3B2
Penguin Books (N.Z.) Ltd, 182–190 Wairau Road,
Auckland 10, New Zealand

Penguin Books Ltd, Registered Offices:
Harmondsworth, Middlesex, England

First published by Signet, an imprint of Dutton Signet,
a division of Penguin Books USA Inc.

First Printing, October, 1995
10 9 8 7 6 5 4 3 2 1

The first chapter of this book appeared in *Dakota Death House*,
the one hundred sixty-fifth volume in this series.

 REGISTERED TRADEMARK—MARCA REGISTRADA

Printed in the United States of America

The Trailsman

Beginnings . . . they bend the tree and they mark the man. Skye Fargo was born when he was eighteen. Terror was his midwife, vengeance his first cry. Killing spawned Skye Fargo, ruthless, cold-blooded murder. Out of the acrid smoke of gunpowder still hanging in the air, he rose, cried out a promise never forgotten.

The Trailsman they began to call him all across the West: searcher, scout, hunter, the man who could see where others only looked, his skills for hire but not his soul, the man who lived each day to the fullest, yet trailed each tomorrow. Skye Fargo, the Trailsman, the seeker who could take the wildness of a land and the wanting of a woman and make them his own.

*1860, the foothills to the
majestic Rockies—where
snow gleamed on the high peaks
above and blood glistened
in the valleys below . . .*

1

Denver was Skye Fargo's kind of town. The watered-down whiskey was cheap, the women who worked the saloons were more than willing, and the local law liked to keep a low profile. Naturally, he made it a point to stop in Denver whenever he was passing through the territory.

On this particular crisp spring evening, Fargo had a giggling blonde in one arm, an almost empty bottle of red-eye in his left hand, and sixty dollars won at stud poker in the pocket of his buckskin shirt. He was halfway to being booze blind, as those who herded cows for a living liked to say, and looking forward to being so drunk by morning he wouldn't be able to find his head with both hands and a map of his anatomy.

Melanie, the fallen dove who had caught the big man's eye back in the saloon where he won the poke, gave him a playful jab in the ribs and asked, "Just where the dickens are you taking me, you handsome devil? I do hope you don't intend to walk me to my door and then give me your hand."

Fargo chuckled lustily. "I had something else in mind."

"Do tell," Melanie said, rubbing her full figure against him, her ripe breasts sliding along his arm like a pair of smooth melons. "I can hardly wait."

Tightening his grip, Fargo hurried her toward the boarding-house where he was staying for a few days. It had been over a week since he last shared his bed with a pretty filly, and he was eager to savor Melanie's charms. His boots clumped heavily on the boardwalk, his spurs jingling merrily with every step.

At the next junction, Fargo turned to the right, onto a quiet side street lined with quaint frame houses, the majority with their lights out. The hour was well past midnight, and here

9

lived some of Denver's more upstanding citizens, devoted churchgoers who typically went to bed before nine o'clock and were up at the crack of dawn.

Fargo slowed so as to make less noise and shushed Melanie into silence. It had not been his intention to stay at the boardinghouse. He would have preferred a hotel. But a convention of drummers was underway, and every last hotel had been filled. A desk clerk at the last one Fargo visited had recommended the boardinghouse, claiming that Miss Dunn, the lady who owned the place, had the softest beds and the best food to be found anywhere.

Fargo had hoped that Miss Dunn would be a pretty young thing worthy of his interest, but she had turned out to be a white-haired spinster as stern as the day was long. "This is a respectable establishment," she had told him, while giving him the sort of look that made him feel as if he were something she would throw out with the dishwater. "I'll stand for no shenanigans. No loud noise. No drinking. And especially no women." She had emphasized that last word. "Is that understood?"

Fargo had mumbled that it was and gone off before she took it into her fussbudget head to check under his fingernails for dirt. He'd gone straight to the nearest saloon, where his luck had taken a wonderful turn for the better. Now all he had to do was sneak Melanie inside, spend the rest of the night in her soft embrace, and sneak her out again in the morning without Miss Erica Dunn being the wiser.

At the rickety white fence framing the brown lawn, Fargo halted. "We can't raise a racket," he cautioned.

"Why?" Melanie asked. "Will your ma paddle you if she catches you sneaking me in?" She found her humor so hilarious that she broke out in a rambunctious cackle.

"Hush up!" Fargo said, stifling her outburst with a hand cupped to her rosy lips. "I'm serious, damn it."

Melanie nodded but kept on chortling to herself as Fargo opened the small gate and stepped along the flagstones to the porch. A board creaked loudly when he set down his right foot. Hesitating, he studied the inky windows. When there was no sign of life within, he tiptoed to the screen door and pulled. The hinges grated like fingernails on a slate, which provoked more chortles from his lady friend.

Making a mental note to never stay in a boardinghouse

again as long as he lived, Fargo opened the inner door. His room was up a flight of stairs and to the right. There was only one other boarder, a store clerk he had seen only briefly.

Taking Melanie's warm hand in his, Fargo crept up the stairs. Although they creaked loudly, he made it to the second floor without waking the landlady. Moving to his door, he gripped the metal latch. Loud snoring could be heard across the hall.

Suddenly Melanie tripped over her own clumsy feet, sprawling against him. Fargo was knocked into the panel. His shoulder hit with a resounding thud. He whirled to steady her and had to control his temper when she gave him a ridiculous grin and tittered at her mistake.

The snoring in the clerk's room broke off, sputtered a full ten seconds, then flared back to full volume.

"You have to watch yourself," Fargo whispered, annoyed. Not at her, but at all the slinking around he had to do. He was a grown man and should have the right to have a woman friend over if he so desired. It galled him to be treated as if he were too young to hold his own britches up.

"I'm trying, lover," Melanie replied huskily, "but with all the coffin varnish I've put down tonight, sometimes it seems as if there's two of everything."

Shaking his head in irritation, Fargo slowly opened the door, then stood aside so that she could enter first.

"My, aren't you the perfect gentleman?" Melanie teased, puckering her mouth at him as she went on by, her long dress swishing against his buckskins.

Fargo followed her, reaching into a pocket for a match so he could light the kerosene lamp. As he passed the edge of the door, he glimpsed movement out of the corner of his left eye. Simultaneously Melanie let out a strident yell.

"Behind you! Look out!"

A heavy object slammed into the side of Fargo's head. Only the fact that he was spinning to confront his attacker saved his life. The blow glanced off his temple instead of caving it in, but the force was still sufficient to stagger him back against an oak dresser.

A bulky shape pounced out of the gloom, a revolver glittering dully in one paw.

Fargo dodged aside as the butt of a pistol smashed down

11

onto the dresser top. Wood chips flew in every direction. The assailant, who wore a floppy hat and a heavy coat, swung again, trying to brain Fargo. Fargo skipped nimbly aside, the unexpected threat clearing his head as quickly as if he had been dunked in a tub of icy water.

"What's going on?" Melanie shouted, retreating toward the far wall. "What is this?"

Fargo had no idea. So far as he knew, he had no enemies in Denver. He assumed the man was a footpad, a thief caught in the act of rifling his room.

In order to end the clash swiftly, Fargo made a grab for his Colt. The man sprang before he could clear leather, and a hand like an iron vise clamped onto Fargo's wrist, keeping him from leveling the pistol. Fargo was borne backward onto the bed. The footpad swung again but Fargo jerked away. The pistol thudded into the mattress instead of Fargo's skull.

Melanie uttered a squawk, then bawled, "Help! Help! For God's sake, someone help us!"

Fargo shifted as the man tried yet again to render him unconscious. He drove a knee into the footpad's groin and the man doubled over, but only for a fleeting instant. Like an uncoiling sidewinder, he lashed out, nearly clipping Fargo across the face. Fargo blocked the blow with a forearm, then rammed a knee into the figure's chest. The man tumbled to the floor.

Leaping to his feet, Fargo started to take snap aim. A boot crashed into his shin. Another caught him in the upper thigh. He was sent tottering toward the wall, toward Melanie, who was so busy yelling at the top of her lungs that she failed to see him. Too late, she tried to jump out of the way. They collided, his legs becoming entangled with hers, and the next he knew, he was on his side, his gun hand pinned under his body, while the footpad was in full flight.

Enraged by the cowardly assault, Fargo shoved Melanie off him and surged erect. He was into the hall in a flash. Framed in the opposite doorway stood the bespectacled store clerk, gaping in amazement.

Heavy footsteps drumming below told Fargo where the thief had gone. He took the stairs three at a time. From the back of the house came angry cries from Miss Dunn, demanding to know the cause of the uproar.

Fargo went out the door in a crouch. It was well he did, for the night blossomed with bright flashes and the booming thunder of three shots. Slugs smacked into the doorjamb. Fargo saw a vague figure vault the picket fence and elevated his Colt to fire, but he never squeezed the trigger. Beyond the fleeing form reared another house. If Fargo missed, innocents might suffer.

Launching himself from the porch, Fargo pounded in pursuit. Once through the gate, he poured on the speed. All along the street, lights blinked on and people were shouting.

Fargo saw the man glance back and veered to the left in case the thief opened fire. Instead, the figure cut across a yard with the speed of a spooked jackrabbit, then around the corner of a small house. Fargo did the same, only he paused at the corner to make sure the man wasn't waiting on the other side for him to show himself.

The stocky shape was now sixty feet off and gaining ground every second.

Acute pain lanced Fargo's head as he resumed pursuit. The pounding he had taken, combined with the effects of the alcohol, were bringing on the granddaddy of all headaches. He found it hard to think. His lungs began to ache, his legs to feel like mush.

Cursing under his breath, Fargo chased his attacker for as long as he could. Nausea brought him to a halt about six blocks from the boardinghouse. By then he could hardly see his quarry.

Fargo leaned on a hitching post in front of a mercantile and struggled to catch his breath. He disliked losing out, but he consoled himself with the thought that at least he had thwarted the thief. Gradually the pangs went away, except for the hammering in his head and an awful bitter taste in his mouth. He needed another drink, but he had dropped the whiskey bottle in the scuffle.

Shoving the Colt into his holster, Fargo trudged toward the Dunn place. The streets were peaceful. A cool breeze wafting off the mountains fanned his face and stirred his long hair. He gulped breaths greedily to combat the lingering effects of the alcohol. It occurred to him that he had been extremely lucky. If he had polished off the whole bottle of rotgut, he would have been in no condition to stop the thief from bashing his brains in.

A murmur of voices greeted Fargo as he neared the boardinghouse, a murmur that swelled in volume the closer he drew. On rounding the last corner he was flabbergasted to see over two dozen citizens, most garbed in nightclothes, clustered in front of the Dunn house. Lamps had been lit up and down the street.

On the porch stood Erica Dunn, in a hot exchange with Melanie Landers. Fargo could hear their words from fifty feet out.

"—you hussy, I won't have your kind in my house! I don't care who invited you upstairs! Mr. Fargo was warned that I won't tolerate that type of behavior."

"What would you know about it, you old prune? And who do you think that you are, calling me a hussy? I'll have you know, I'm as respectable as you are. At least I don't lure men into my house under the pretense of renting rooms to them."

Fargo saw the spinster cock a fist. He shoved through the crowd and dashed up the walk just in time to grab Melanie and keep her from scratching the landlady's eyes out. Holding the dove at arm's length, he declared, "Now hold on, you two. This is no way for a pair of ladies to be acting."

"How dare you call this tart a lady!" Miss Dunn sniffed.

Melanie wriggled and strained, trying to break free. "I'm more of a lady than you'll ever be, you withered old hag." She took a swing that missed. "Call me names again and you'll be picking your head up off the ground!"

"Now, now," Fargo chided, for lack of anything better to say. He had to hold Miss Dunn at bay. She was purple with fury and kept trying to punch Melanie. "If anyone has cause to be upset here, it's me. I'm the one that thief tried to rob."

Erica Dunn stepped back. "What thief? What happened, anyway? All this scarlet woman would say is that someone was waiting for you in your room."

In the crowd rose a deep voice. "I'd like to hear the answer to that my own self." From out of their midst stalked a lanky man in jeans and a nightshirt. A gun belt seemed out of place draped around his narrow hips, but right in keeping with the flashy tin star pinned to his skinny chest. He advanced to the edge of the porch and regarded Fargo coldly. "What in the world is going on, Erica? All that shooting woke me out of a sound sleep, and I put in a mighty long day."

14

"Don't ask me, Marshal Fedder," Erica answered. "I was sleeping soundly, too, when there was this terrible ruckus. Yelling, shots, you name it. About scared the living daylights out of me, I tell you."

A spindly specimen wearing glasses materialized in the doorway and jabbed an accusing finger at Fargo. "It was him, Marshal. There was a fight in his room, then all this gunplay out here. Right in the heart of town, too!"

"Thanks for the information, Tim," the law dog said in friendly fashion. "But I reckon I know the layout of Denver as well as you do." His friendliness evaporated when he swiveled toward Fargo. "Who are you, stranger, and what are you doing in our neck of the woods?"

Fargo told his name, adding, "I've passed through Denver lots of times, and never had anyone try to steal my effects until now. I chased the bastard, but never got a good look at him."

The owner of the house put a pale hand to her wrinkled throat. "What language! I had no idea you were so uncouth, or I never would have let a room to you."

"Sorry, ma'am." Fargo wanted to stay on her good side. "You can't blame me for being a bit flustered. That man came close to caving my skull."

Marshal Fedder swung toward the crowd. "You can go home now, folks. Everything is under control. I'll handle the rest if you don't mind." Waving an arm, he shooed them along, and when the last couple had drifted into the night, he indicated the screen door. "Now why don't we go inside, Erica? I'd like to see this man's room and hear the whole story from start to finish."

Miss Dunn's robe had fallen open during her argument with Melanie. She just now noticed and quickly pulled it tight, her cheeks flushing crimson. "Whatever you want, Marshal. I'll fix a fresh pot of coffee if you'd like."

"I wouldn't want to put you to any trouble," Fedder said.

"Fiddlesticks. It's no bother at all."

Fargo entered last. He had no hankering to spend the next hour or so answering a lot of useless questions, but he couldn't come right out and refuse or the lawman might see fit to haul him off to the jail. Melanie gave him a longing look, which he returned, and when no one was looking, she blew him a little kiss. She was a spunky one, that was for sure.

The clerk chattered like a chipmunk all the way to the second floor. "It was awful, Marshal, just awful. There I was, sleeping like a newborn babe, dreaming of the time I sold nine bolts of cloth in one day, when I was torn from my slumber by loud thuds and thumps and yells. I got up to investigate and was nearly plowed over by someone running from Mr. Fargo's room. Then Mr. Fargo dashed out, holding a gun. A gun, mind you! It was enough to give a man a conniption."

"I'm sure it was." Marshal Fedder demonstrated the patience of a saint. "But it's all over. You go back to sleep while I do my job."

The clerk reluctantly obeyed, curling a lip at Fargo as he did.

There were times, such as this, when Fargo sorely regretted having to utilize civilized accommodations. He'd much rather sleep out under the stars than have to put up with the sort of things he had gone through in the past fifteen minutes.

Fargo made no protest as the lawman conducted a search of the room. He noticed the puzzled look that etched Fedder's face, a look that deepened the longer the marshal searched.

"Didn't you tell me that the man you scared off was trying to steal your things?"

"That would be my guess," Fargo answered.

"Then why didn't he touch any of your belongings?" Marshal Fedder wondered. "Your saddlebags are closed, your bedroll hasn't been unrolled, even that fine Sharps in the corner was left right where it is."

"Maybe we surprised him before he could take anything," Melanie chimed in from the corridor.

"Or maybe he didn't give a tinker's damn about your possessions," Fedder said to Fargo. "He might have been after you."

Fargo shook his head. "Hardly likely. I don't know of anyone in Denver who is out to get me. The only ones I told my name to are Miss Dunn and Miss Landers, and neither of them has any cause to kill me."

The tin star cracked a grin. "I wouldn't lay money on Erica being any too friendly after what happened. She's liable to toss you out on your ear." Striding to the window, he peered out at the narrow street. "If by some miracle she doesn't, I'd advise you to keep a chair propped against your door until morning.

If anyone tries to break in, give a holler. I live only two doors down and I'm a light sleeper."

Now Fargo knew how the lawman had arrived on the scene so promptly. "If someone really is after my hide, I'll do more than holler." He patted his Colt to stress the point.

"Just so no innocent bystanders are caught in the cross fire," Marshal Fedder said. "I won't abide having the people who put me in office harmed in any way." Moving to the door, he went to touch his hat brim and blinked when he realized he wasn't wearing one. "I'll go see if I can calm Erica down."

"You'd do that for me?" Fargo asked. He was grateful that the lawman wasn't going to pester him with questions.

"For you and me, both," Fedder said. "I don't want her showing up on my doorstep at first light demanding to swear out a complaint. I like to sleep in until seven or so." Pivoting on a boot heel, he was about to leave when he drew up short and snapped his fingers. "Your name is Fargo? Why didn't I remember sooner!"

"Remember what?" Fargo asked.

Fedder glanced over his shoulder. "I've heard of you, mister. A lot of people have. Including a woman who came into my office about a week ago. Prim snip of a gal, pretty as a butterfly and as polite as could be. She wanted to know if I had any idea where she could find you. When I told her no, she was real disappointed. Asked me to keep an eye out for you and to let her know if you showed up."

"This woman have a name?"

"Felicia Taugner. She was staying at the Imperial Hotel over on Fourth Street, but I don't know if she's still there. You might want to check in the morning."

"I'll do that. Thanks." Fargo moved to the door to usher the lawman out. He was anxious to get Melanie into his bed. He could hardly wait to get her snug under the blankets, to feel her smooth skin under his probing hands. Then he saw Erica Dunn materialize at the top of the stairs.

"The coffee is about ready, Marshal. Come on down." Her flinty gaze settled on the dove. "As for you, young lady, I'll thank you to leave these premises this second."

"But—," Melanie began.

"Don't argue!" the landlady snapped. "This is my house,

and I can do as I darn well please. If I don't want you here, you'll have to go. It's my legal right, isn't it, Marshal?"

"Yes, ma'am," Fedder said, frowning.

Melanie gave Fargo a helpless look of disappointment, her shapely shoulders drooping. "Darn. I had my hopes set on having a little fun." She moved to go past Dunn, but stopped, brightening. "There's always my place, Skye. It's a rat hole compared to here, but no one can toss us out."

The suggestion suited Fargo. In the morning he would return for his things and head on out of town. "I'd like that," he said. He went to join her, stopping in surprise when the lawman blocked his path.

"Are you sure that's such a wise idea?"

Fargo was all set to brush on by and to let the tin star know he should mind his own business when Fedder's meaning hit him like a brick between the eyes. The whiskey had befuddled his senses to the point where he had failed to see the danger to Melanie if she stayed in his company. Should the lawman be right, should someone actually be gunning for him, whoever it was might just try again. "No, I guess it's not," he said softly.

"What?" Melanie said, sounding hurt.

"You run along," Fargo forced himself to say. "I'd better stay by myself tonight."

Melanie was genuinely upset and it showed. "I thought you were different than most. I thought we could have a grand time together." In a swirl of red, she was gone, her shoes clacking noisily all the way to the front walk.

"You did the right thing," Marshal Fedder said.

"Did I?" Fargo responded, stepping to the window. He saw Melanie, arms clasped to her bosom, dash out into the street and bear to the right. He also saw something else—a bulky shadow that detached itself from the house across the street and stalked into the dark after her.

2

Skye Fargo spun and dashed from the bedroom, barreling past a surprised Fedder and one very startled landlady. "I think the son of a bitch is after Melanie," he declared as he bounded down the stairs.

Fargo didn't wait for the marshal to catch up. He slammed out through the doors on the fly, slanted across the lawn, and hurtled the fence in a long, high leap. Half a block away, a pair of dusky figures struggled in the middle of the otherwise deserted street. A woman's low cries carried on the breeze, mixed with the gruff curses of her assailant.

Palming the Colt, Fargo ran for all he was worth. He hoped to get closer before the attacker spotted him. The man was pounding on Melanie with both fists, pummeling her into the ground. The poor woman was either too scared or too dazed to scream.

Fargo mentally measured the yards he had to cover. Twenty were all that remained, then eighteen, fifteen—and the stocky man glanced up. A gun flashed into view and spat lead and smoke. Fargo had already thrown himself to the right. The slug missed. Fargo returned fire, thumbing the hammer twice, his trigger finger closing smoothly.

At the second blast, the stocky man jerked around as if struck. But he recovered immediately, seized Melanie with his other hand, and pulled her erect in front of him, turning her into a living shield.

Fargo promptly halted and crouched to present a smaller target. He wasn't about to blaze away and have her suffer the consequences. The man in the floppy hat was backpedaling rapidly toward a building, bent low so that only the hat and the top of his face showed. Fargo saw him point the revolver and coiled to leap aside.

"You there! Stop! This is the marshal!"

The bulky figure swung toward the approaching lawman and banged off a shot that caused Fedder to dive to the earth. The marshal raised his gun but held his fire.

Tense moments elapsed. The gunman reached the building and paused. He said something in Melanie's ear, then shoved her hard and darted around the corner.

Both Fargo and Fedder raced to the stricken woman. As much as Fargo wanted to get his hands on the scum who had beaten her, he waved the lawman on and knelt by her side. "How bad is it?" he asked, gently touching her shoulder.

Melanie slowly rolled over. Tears poured from under her quivering eyelids, and her shoulders shook with each quiet sob. Even in the dark it was apparent she had been battered badly. Blood smeared her face and chin, trickling from a nasty gash over her right eye and another high on her left cheek. "I hurt inside something terrible," she said, quaking. "He hit me in the stomach a few times."

Fargo replaced the Colt, clasped her hand, and braced an arm under her back. She sat up with his help, then sagged against him, weeping softly, her once lustrous hair disheveled, her dress rumpled and torn in several spots. "Can you stand?"

"I'll try."

Her legs buckled when Fargo raised her halfway up. He had to hold tight to keep her from falling. Melanie buried her face in his shirt and cried harder, her fingers digging into his broad shoulders for support. Only after she had cried herself out, her sobs tapering to pitiable whines and sniffles, did he turn her toward the boardinghouse. Landlady or no landlady, he was going to do what he could for her.

Much to Fargo's surprise, Erica Dunn made no protest. She took one look at the dove's bloody features and said, rather tenderly, "Take her into the sitting room and place her on the settee. I'll bring hot water and towels."

"I'd be obliged," Fargo said.

"And don't look so shocked, young man," Miss Dunn said as she held the doors for him. "I might be strict about the rules

20

I impose, but I won't stand by and let another human being suffer."

Melanie opened her eyes when Fargo set her down and grasped at his sleeve. "Don't leave me," she said.

"I wasn't about to," he assured her.

"That horrible man—," Melanie said, and shuddered.

"Don't talk about him if it bothers you so," Fargo advised. Procuring a pillow from the other end of the settee, he slid it under her head so she would be more comfortable.

Melanie mustered a wan smile and reached up to touch him. "You're sweet, do you know that?"

"I've been called a lot of things, but never that before." Fargo eased onto the cushion beside her.

"That man, he wanted to know about you."

"Did he mention me by name?"

The dove nodded, the movement making her wince. "He snuck up behind me and caught me before I could run off. I told him that I didn't have any money, and he told me that he didn't want any. All he wanted was information on you."

"Did he say why?"

"No. I explained that I hardly knew you, that we had just met this evening, and it made him so mad he started beating me. It all happened so fast, there was nothing I could do. Thank God you came along when you did or he might have killed me."

Melanie's voice broke, and Fargo soothed her by stroking her brow while being careful not to brush the bruises and welts marking her fair skin. The news troubled him, for it meant the lawman had been right and someone was out to get him. But who could it be? he mused. He hadn't been in town long enough to make any new enemies. "Did he say anything else? Any clues as to who he is or what he's about?"

"No," Melanie replied. "But I did get the impression he's not the kind to give up easily. You should have seen his eyes, Skye. They reminded me of the eyes of a rattler I once saw, flat, and cold as driven snow—only his were pale blue."

"What about the color of his hair?" Fargo fished for a description.

"Sandy, I would say, although not much of it stuck out from under that big hat of his." Melanie thought a moment. "He did have a tiny scar on the point of his chin, as if a knife nicked him once. And one of his fingers was bent all wrong."

"Bent how?"

"Crooked, like. I saw it when he was poking me in the chest. Instead of being straight, the end of the finger bends upward. I guess it broke once and was never set properly."

Sandy hair, a scar, and a busted finger. They weren't much to go on, but they might be enough to enable Fargo to track the gunman down. A few dollars under the table did wonders for the memory of most bartenders and desk clerks.

A dress rustled behind them, and in walked Erica Dunn, carrying a tray laden with a pile of small white towels and a basin of steaming water. "I'll fix her up, Mr. Fargo. You run along until I get done. Women need their privacy at a time like this, you know."

Fargo knew the landlady was going to check Melanie over thoroughly. "She was hit in the stomach," he mentioned so Miss Dunn would know to probe for signs of internal bleeding. Going out, he closed the sliding door and walked to the porch.

Marshal Fedder was just coming up the street. He kicked the gate open and limped up to the wooden steps. His expression showed how he had fared. "The bastard got clean away. I almost had him, until he went down the bank behind the stable. Damned if I didn't slip and sprain my ankle."

"It couldn't be helped," Fargo said.

"Yes, it could," the law dog groused. "I'm not the man I once was. Sitting behind a desk most of the time has been the ruin of my health." He paused. "The odds are that he's still in Denver. Whoever he is, he must want you pretty badly."

"I wonder," Fargo said. "He could have shot me earlier, when I entered my room, but all he did was try to knock me out. And he had another chance to kill me when he was backing off with Melanie, yet he didn't."

"Maybe you're misreading him. He fired at you, remember? I saw him."

"And he missed. If he couldn't hit me at that close range, he's either the worst shot this side of the Rockies or he deliberately missed me."

"You hit him, though, didn't you?"

"I winged him, I think. But even then he didn't try to gun me down."

Marshal Fedder shook his head in exasperation. "It makes no sense to me, and I've been wearing a badge for over twelve years." He jabbed a thumb at the house. "How's the whore?"

"In a bad way. Miss Dunn is with her now."

"Should I fetch a sawbones?"

"Let's wait and see."

Their wait wasn't long. Within five minutes the landlady appeared, a damp towel draped over her shoulder. "She has a lot of bruises, and she'll be black and blue for a spell, but she'll live. She can thank her Maker you rushed out when you did, Mr. Fargo. That dreadful man beat on her head and then started working his way lower. He must be a despicable brute."

"He'll be a dead brute once I get my hands on him," Fargo vowed.

The marshal perked up. "I won't have anyone taking the law into their own hands in my town," he declared. "If you find the vermin, you're to notify me. Savvy?"

A grunt sufficed as Fargo's answer. He had no intention of making a promise he wouldn't keep. Whoever was causing him so much trouble was going to learn the hard way that when push came to shove, he could shove as hard as the next man, if not harder. "If Melanie is fit enough," he offered, "I'll take her home now."

"Rubbish. You'll do no such thing, young man," the landlady said. "That poor girl is comfortable right where she is, and she's perfectly welcome to stay as long as she needs to. Never let it be said that Erica Dunn doesn't know the meaning of compassion." Wiping her hands on the towel, she nodded farewell at the lawman and went in.

"That's my cue, I reckon," Fedder said. "I'll be by tomorrow to ask you a few more questions."

"I should be here," Fargo said glumly. After looking forward to Melanie's company, he was disappointed at the turn of events. The last thing he wanted was to spend the night alone, yet that's exactly how he did spend it, tossing and turning under the sheet in restless frustration until shortly before dawn.

Always an early riser anyway, in this instance Fargo was dressed and quietly closing the front door behind him as a cock crowed somewhere to the south. The saloons were all closed, which meant he must delay his hunt for the stocky man until later.

But hotels were open. The tired desk clerk at the modestly decorated Imperial looked up from the large ledger he was scribbling in and tried to stifle a yawn. "Good morning, sir. How may I be of service?"

"Is there a lady staying here by the name of Felicia Taugner?" Fargo asked. During the night the thought had struck him that perhaps there was a link between the woman who had visited the marshal and the gunman. It was an avenue worth checking out.

"That we do," the man said without having to consult the names of the guests. "Miss Taugner has been in room 107 for over a week and a half." He paused to study Fargo from head to toe, the corner of his mouth curling upward in ill-concealed distaste. "May I inquire what your business is with her at this ungodly hour?"

"You may not," Fargo said, hastening down the hallway.

"Hold on!" the clerk exclaimed, rushing around the counter. "It's my job to insure that our guests, particularly our female guests, aren't disturbed unless they want to be. I'll have to ask you to leave and come back at a more reasonable time."

"I need to see her now." Fargo refused to be cowed. He had taken only two more steps when the clerk scooted in front of him and pushed against his chest.

"I really must insist," the man said. "For all I know, you mean to do her harm."

"Not her. You," Fargo said, and planted his right fist in the busybody's gut. Most pencil pushers would have buckled then and there, but this one was made of stouter stuff and weakly tried to land a haymaker. Fargo swatted the blow aside, grabbed the front of the man's white shirt, and thrust him up against the wall. "Where are you from, mister?" he demanded.

"From?" the clerk sputtered, confused. "Philadelphia. Why? What difference does that make?"

"I thought so. Your accent gave you away," Fargo said. "Out here folks don't take kindly to people who meddle in

24

their affairs. Some men would shoot you for what you just did, but I don't aim to waste good lead just because you happen to fancy Miss Taugner."

The man reacted as if he'd been caught with his hands in the cookie jar. "Fancy her? Where did you ever get a harebrained idea like that? I hardly know the lady."

"There must be fifty rooms in this hotel, and every one is filled. I know, because I stopped by yesterday, trying to get one," Fargo said as he let go and stepped back. "All those guests, yet you didn't look up her name when I asked about her room. Why? Because you already knew. Because you've watched her come and go and wished you could screw up the courage to ask her out."

Almost comical astonishment claimed the desk clerk. "What are you? One of those mind readers I've heard about?"

There were those who believed that Skye Fargo was the best tracker who ever lived. He could trail anything, anywhere, it was claimed. It was true that he had devoted countless hours to learning to read prints of all sizes and shapes, so that now he could do so with the same ease with which most men read books. But that had been only a small part of his wilderness education. To survive in the untamed mountains and out on the vast prairie, he had to be able to read men, too, to guess the hidden motives behind their actions, to tell his enemies from his friends. It was a skill that also came in handy when confronted by bumbling desk clerks. "No, I'm a sign reader," Fargo said, and walked off, hiding his grin.

The room was on the left, near the end of the hall. Fargo rapped once, lightly. When there was no response, he knocked harder, and this time was rewarded with the sound of a bedspring squeaking and the scrape of a chair, perhaps made by someone lifting a robe off the back of it.

"Who's there?" The voice was feminine and frail, laced with a faint tinge of fear. "Who is it? What do you want?"

"I understand you were asking about me, ma'am. The name is Skye Fargo."

The fear was replaced by excitement. "I'd about given up hope! Please wait a minute. I'll be right with you."

Fargo leaned against the wall and folded his arms. He could hear her scurrying about the room, making herself presentable.

Outside, a golden crown framed a sky the same hue as his lake-blue eyes. Soon the whole town would be up and about. And somewhere out there was the man Fargo was going to find, even if it took a month of Sundays.

A rasping click sounded and the door was yanked inward. There stood an attractive snip of a woman, just as the lawman had described her. Small of build, with angular features, she nonetheless had a crystal-smooth complexion, hair like polished coal, and a pair of breasts that could have doubled as watermelons. But to keep any man from getting the wrong idea, she had thrown on a black dress that covered her from chin to feet. "After all this time," she said. "We meet at last."

"You can thank Marshal Fedder. He's the one who told me that you were looking for me," Fargo said, removing his hat. "Mind if I come in, Miss Taugner? I'd like to learn why."

Without hesitation, Felicia stepped aside and bade him enter. She closed the door, then stepped to a chest of drawers on which rested a large handbag. "I'm so glad you received word. In another few days they'll arrive, and they'll be so disappointed if I don't have a guide lined up by then."

"They?" Fargo said. He noticed an old trunk in a corner and another faded black dress in a closet. She wasn't a wealthy woman, by any means.

"Oh, I'm sorry. I should start at the beginning, I suppose, and explain everything," Felicia said, betraying a case of nerves as she took a seat and fidgeted to get comfortable.

"That would be nice," Fargo said. He imagined that she was flustered at being roused from bed so early, and he didn't blame her. He really shouldn't have let his impatience get the better of him.

"Well, let's see. I'm a schoolteacher, Mr. Fargo. Until recently I was employed at the Brighton Academy in Boston, Massachusetts, an exclusive school for young ladies of social prominence."

"A school for rich snots," Fargo translated.

Felicia Taugner behaved like someone who had just swallowed a frog. She gaped, squirmed uncomfortably, clasped her hands together until the knuckles were white, and swallowed hard. "My goodness. Frontiersmen are a blunt lot, aren't they?" She paused, and when Fargo made no reply, she went on. "Anyway, I've been offered a job north of here. So have two other teachers due to arrive in Denver in three days. I was given the task of finding someone to escort us to our destination. When I asked around, I was told that you are a fine scout with a sterling reputation."

"Hold it right there," Fargo cut in. "I don't mean to be rude, but why are you wasting my time? Yes, I scout. Mostly for the army, or for wagon trains heading through Indian country." He paced over to the window and gazed at the rising sun. "Taking three schoolmarms for a little jaunt in the country is hardly my line of work."

"I wouldn't call a journey of over four hundred miles a little jaunt," Felicia said testily.

Fargo forgot all about the glorious sunrise. "Where in the world are you headed? Canada?"

"Not quite," Felicia answered dryly. "Have you ever heard of the Bighorn Mountains?"

Nodding, Fargo said, "I've been through that stretch of the country a few times. It's no fit place for a lady like yourself. There are hostiles all over, and grizzlies and mountain lions to worry about."

The schoolmarm wasn't flustered. "East of the Bighorns three settlements have taken root. Perhaps you know of them, too?"

"Banner, Wyarno, and Bighorn," Fargo recited. They barely qualified as settlements, in his opinion. Between the three of them they couldn't boast of more than a hundred and fifty souls, mostly hardy ranchers and farmers. Many were married couples, though, with large broods needing an education.

Felicia nodded. "The good people of those settlements intend to see their communities grow and prosper. Each has built a small schoolhouse. They pooled their resources and advertised for teachers. I answered Banner's ad. My colleagues responded to those placed by Wyarno and Bighorn. It's been arranged for all three of us to travel together. All we lack is a guide." She beamed prettily. "A scout, if you will."

Fargo pursed his lips and pondered. The three settlements were located close to one another about ten miles east of the center of the Bighorn range. The region was smack in the middle of territory the Sioux roamed. And now and then the Blackfeet made raids into the area. It was no place for a naive Easterner who had never killed anything bigger than a fly in her whole life. Or was he being too quick to judge? "Have you ever killed anyone, ma'am?"

If the last time she had swallowed a frog, this time it was a rump roast. "Mercy me! What kind of question is that? No, I've never killed anyone, and I hope to heaven I never have to. Why would you even ask?"

"Because if the Blackfeet or Sioux swoop down on your party before you reach those settlements, that's what you'll have to do to stay alive. Unless a warrior takes a shine to you and totes you back to his lodge to be his wife."

"You're deliberately trying to scare me, Mr. Fargo, and it won't work. Do you see these?" Felicia pulled a handful of envelopes from her bag. "These are all from ladies of standing in Banner. Ladies who in some cases have lived there for several years without ever setting eyes on a savage. They assure me that I'll be perfectly safe."

"The only reason the Sioux have left them alone is because so far the whites have fought shy of the Black Hills. But sooner or later some fool is going to set foot there and all hell will break loose. The Sioux won't stand for having their sacred ground violated."

"That tone you just used. It almost sounds as if you'd side with the savages against the whites."

"I spent time with the Sioux when I was younger. I know how they think," Fargo detailed.

"Why, that's even better. If we meet any along the way, you can convince them we're friendly." Felicia Taugner rose. "So what do you say? Will you accept the offer? I've been authorized to pay you two hundred dollars."

The money was a pittance compared to what Fargo usually made. "I'll have to think it over," he hedged, moving to the door. His hand on the latch, he looked at her. "One other thing. Do you happen to know a stocky man with sandy hair, a scar on his chin, and a crippled finger? A man partial to a floppy hat and a big coat?"

"No. Why? Should I?"

"No, ma'am," Fargo said. "I'll be in touch soon." Striding into the hall, he drew up short on seeing someone approach. It was a stocky man with sandy hair, a scar on his chin, and a crippled finger, a man who wore a floppy brown hat and an oversized wool coat.

3

It was hard to say who was more surprised, Fargo or the man in the floppy hat. The gunman had been making note of room numbers as he advanced along the hall, but on seeing Fargo he whirled and sped toward the lobby as if fire nipped at his heels.

Fargo didn't waste his breath shouting for the man to stop. He simply drew the Colt and sped in pursuit, confident that this time the cutthroat wouldn't get away. Although he had a clear shot, Fargo didn't take it. He had never been a back shooter. And the gunman was making no move to unlimber his own hardware.

Swiftly Fargo gained. The hard frontier life had made whip-cords of his muscles; he was much more fit than most. A mere three strides separated them when an elderly man stepped from a room ahead, turned in their direction, and stood riveted in place in consternation.

The wily gunman was not one to let an opportunity pass him by. He seized the guest, spun, and shoved the man with all his might.

Fargo tried to get out of the way but he was going too fast. He did take a half step to the right, and that's when the shocked guest crashed into him. The impact smashed them against the wall. He tried to push free and continue the chase, but the older man clung to him in a daze.

Meanwhile the gunman gained the lobby and slowed briefly to look back. His mocking smirk was meant to aggravate.

"Let go, damn it!" Fargo said, trying to untangle himself. The other man stepped back, a hand to his chest. Fargo went on and was only a few feet from the end of the corridor when the desk clerk, apparently curious about all the commotion, stepped directly into his path.

"Look out!" Fargo cried, but it was too late. The man had the reflexes of a petrified tortoise. Fargo hit him going at his top speed and the two of them went tumbling across the floor, scattering several chairs.

A sharp pain lanced Fargo's side as he shoved to his feet. A glance showed the clerk wheezing and sputtering but otherwise unharmed, so he dashed to the entrance and flung open the wide door.

Few people were abroad so early. Down the street a mule skinner was hitching his team. The proprietor of a dry goods store was sweeping off the walk in front of his place. Elsewhere a man emptied spittoons at the side of a saloon. Nowhere was there any sign of the elusive gunman.

"Damn it all," Fargo grumbled, going back in. He reached the clerk in time to assist the man into a chair. "The one I was after, have you ever seen him before?"

"No," the clerk mumbled while touching himself to see if he was still in one piece.

"Are you sure? He's never been in the hotel?"

"Not to my knowledge." The clerk sat up. "Why? Who is he? Why were you after him?"

"Remember what I told you about minding your own business?" Fargo was all set to leave when he saw Miss Felicia Taugner appear. She came over, her hands primly clasped at her slim waist.

"I thought I heard a ruckus in the hall, and when I looked out, I saw you run into Mr. Edwards here. I trust that you're all right?"

"Just dandy," Fargo said. "I saw that man I mentioned. Strange, isn't it, that he shows up in your hotel, outside your room?"

"What are you implying, sir?"

"Not a thing, lady," Fargo said, when the truth was that the incident had made him highly suspicious of her. It had to be more than mere coincidence, the gunman showing up when and where he did. Either she knew the man and was lying, or the gunman had shadowed him from the boardinghouse. He should have paid more attention on the way over. "I'll be see-

31

ing you." he turned to depart, stopping when she said his name.

"If it turns out that you decide to decline my job offer, perhaps you would be so kind as to recommend someone else. There must be any number of competent men in Denver who could guide us to the settlements."

"There are a lot of competent men," Fargo allowed, "but finding a competent scout is another matter. Most stick to established trails when they travel. Men who have crossed Indian country and lived to tell about it are few and far between."

"There must be a road we can take," Felicia said. "One of my correspondents mentioned hauling her goods from Denver in a wagon."

"That they did," Fargo said. "And they still make regular trips to Denver for supplies, five to ten wagons at a time, along with a dozen armed men." He shook his head. "There's no road there, though. They just head north along the foothills until they reach the Medicine Bow Range, and from there they cut due north across hundreds of miles of open plain to the Bighorns."

Edwards had been listening intently. "Do you plan to travel all that way with this man, Miss Taugner?" he said. "After seeing how he behaves and all?"

Fargo pivoted. "What's that supposed to mean?"

"Nothing. Nothing whatsoever," Edwards declared much too hastily. "I was just trying to point out that such a journey would be very dangerous, especially for a dainty woman like her."

"For once we agree on something," Fargo said. Nodding at the schoolmarm, he strode out, saying, "Like I told you, I'll give it some thought. If I decide not to go, I'll try and rustle up someone you can trust."

"I would be so terribly grateful," Felicia said.

Edwards was giving her cow eyes when Fargo looked back. He closed the door and crossed the street at an angle to a restaurant just opening up for the day. A portly man wearing a greasy apron greeted him and indicated a long bench along the right wall.

Fargo was in a bear of a mood. He had a hunch there was a

lot more to the schoolmarm business than petite Felicia Taugner had let on. And he disliked being made a fool of, which the gunman had done twice. Combined with the pounding his head had taken the night before and his lack of sleep, he was cranky enough to eat nails.

Instead, Fargo settled for a heaping plate of bacon and eggs and a side order of six thick flapjacks covered with thick, rich maple syrup. He washed it all down with five cups of black coffee. By the time he was done, he was in a better frame of mind. But it only lasted until he strolled outside. The sun felt warm on his back and he idly stretched, gazing at the Imperial.

Walking from the hotel, linked arm in arm, were Felicia and Edwards, the desk clerk. He was grinning like a kid who had just been granted his heart's desire, while she wore the same reserved mask she always did. They headed away from the restaurant, the clerk gushing words like a geyser gushed water.

Fargo didn't know what to make of it. Edwards had claimed he hardly knew her, yet there they were, acting like the best of friends. Fargo had half a mind to go over and question them, but after lecturing the clerk on minding one's own business, he couldn't very well poke his nose into their affairs.

The big man shrugged and made for the boardinghouse. He took a roundabout route, stopping often to check if he was being trailed. At the stable nearest the Dunn house, he paid his Ovaro a visit and dawdled to rub the stallion down and fork a pile of hay into its stall.

There was a surprise waiting for him on the front porch of the boardinghouse in the form of Marshal Fedder. The lawman sat on the railing, his white hat pushed back, his badge gleaming in the sunlight. He was in the act of rolling a cigarette. "Howdy, Fargo."

"Are you here to check up on Melanie?"

"No, I came to see you." Fedder licked the paper and shaped it around the tobacco. "I couldn't get to sleep after I went home, so I got up early and paid a visit to a few folks I know who like to keep their ears close to the ground."

"And?"

"The word is that the hombre we tangled with isn't alone. He has five or six friends, and they all work for a fancy Easterner who is staying at the Summit House."

Fargo whistled. The Summit House was the single most expensive hotel in the whole town, frequented by those with money to burn. Prospectors who had struck it rich, speculators from east of the Mississippi, politicians and the like, they were its usual clientele.

"My sentiments exactly," Fedder said, clamping the corner of his mouth on the cigarette. "I thought I'd mosey on over and have a few words with the gentleman. If you're inclined, you're welcome to tag along. But if you see the gent we're after, you're to let me handle him."

"I've already seen him once today," Fargo said, and related his visit to the Imperial.

"Whoever he is, he's mighty interested in your doings," the lawman stated. "If it was me, I'd be almighty curious to learn why."

"Count me in."

The Summit House was located at the corner of Broadway and Pioneer Street. Stepping from the hot, dusty street into the cool, lavish interior was like stepping into another world. Luxurious carpet covered the floor, large paintings decorated the walls, and an immense, glittering chandelier hung over the mahogany front desk.

A trim clerk attired in an immaculate suit looked up and did a double take. "Marshal. It isn't often that we see you in our wonderful establishment. To what do we owe the honor?"

"Spare me the cow crap, Brice," Fedder said. "I stepped in enough of it back on the farm." He tapped the gold-trimmed register. "I hear tell that you have a dude staying here by the name of Morgan. Frederick Morgan."

"That we do," Brice confirmed. "He and his entourage have been here several days now. They've taken our very best suite." Brice leaned forward to whisper confidentially. "He can afford it, too. He's made a fortune in the import business."

"I'd like to see him."

"Is this official business?"

"What difference does it make? Give me his room number."

Brice curled his mouth in a slick smile. "I'm afraid I can't let you go barging in on him unless you have a very good reason. You know the policy here, Marshal. The welfare of our customers always comes first."

Fargo barely saw the lawman's arm move, but one second it was resting on the edge of the counter and the next Fedder had the clerk in an iron grip and was throttling him.

"Now you listen, and you listen good, you cocky jackass. So long as I'm wearing this badge I can go any damn place I want, any damn time I want. And right this minute I want to talk with Frederick Morgan. So give me his room number before I see fit to toss you into the hoosegow until you learn some respect for the law."

Brice was gulping for air. He stepped back when released and rubbed his red neck. "I didn't mean to offend you," he spluttered. "Of course I'll help in any way. The management of the Summit House is always happy to cooperate with duly appointed legal authorities."

Only then did Fargo realize the man was more than an ordinary clerk. He made no comment as they were given directions to stairs that took them to the third floor and a door bearing a gold star. At the lawman's knock, it swung inward to reveal a massive black man wearing a suit of the same color.

"Marshal Fedder to see Mr. Morgan," the law dog said. "And I won't take no for an answer."

"One moment," the black man said, closing the door.

Fedder nudged Fargo. "Remember what I told you. No causing trouble. I'll do the talking and whatever else needs to be done. If you can't abide by that, you might as well skedaddle."

"It's fine by me," Fargo said.

Again the door opened. The black giant smiled and beckoned. "Enter please, sirs. Mr. Morgan is waiting for you."

Fedder hooked his thumbs in his gun belt. "Who the hell are you, sonny? His butler?"

"No, sir," the black said calmly. "Mr. Morgan likes to call me one of his associates, so I guess that's what I am."

A sitting room afforded a panoramic vista of Denver. Ringed around it, standing as if awaiting instructions, were four men. In a high-backed chair that looked more like a throne sat Frederick Morgan himself.

Fargo had met rich Easterners before. The majority had been pampered weaklings who couldn't last five minutes in the wild on their own. This man was the exception to the rule.

Over six feet in height, endowed with powerful shoulders and a face that might have been sculpted from granite, Frederick Morgan had the air of a grizzly about him. His piercing green eyes locked on Fargo and the marshal and scrutinized them closely. Fargo had the impression that Morgan noted all there was worth knowing about him with that probing look, but of course such a notion was nonsense.

"Marshal Fedder, I believe?" the businessman said in a booming voice as he rose and extended a hand fit for a lumberjack.

"You know me?" the lawman said, shaking hands.

"Of you," Morgan amended. "I make it a point to learn all the pertinent facts I can about any town I stay in." He gestured at a pair of vacant easy chairs. "Please, have a seat. Would either of you care for refreshments? Drinks, perhaps?"

"No, thanks," Fedder said.

Fargo could tell the marshal had been taken aback. Fedder was accustomed to dealing with businessmen who were small potatoes compared to the notable visitor before them. Fargo shook his head when Morgan glanced at him and noticed how Morgan's stare lingered.

"What can I do for you, then?"

Fedder looked around the room. "I'm sorry to bother you this way, but I've been told that you have a man working for you who answers the description of a troublemaker I'm after."

"I'm shocked," Morgan said, not sounding shocked at all. "The people I hire are the best around. They know better than to sully my reputation by getting into difficulty with the law." Manicured fingers stroked his silk tie. "Do you know this person's name?"

"I wish I did," Fedder said, then supplied a description of the gunman in the floppy brown hat. "At the very least he's guilty of assault and discharging a firearm within the town limits. Depending on what he has to say for himself, he could also be charged with attempted murder."

"How distressing that such individuals are allowed to run around loose in your fair town," Morgan said. "Or should I say your fair city? I understand that next year the Territorial Assembly intends to incorporate Denver."

"Where did you hear that?"

"I have my sources." Morgan opened a silver cigar box and took out a cigar the size of a banana. "As for your source of information, I'm afraid they are mistaken. I have no one answering the description you gave in my employ. If I did, I would turn him over to you myself."

While the two men talked, Fargo had been studying the other four on the sly. They weren't the sort of hired help the average businessman had in his employ.

For starters there was the tall drink of water leaning against the wall. The man wore a wide-brimmed black hat, a gray suit with a white shirt, and had a nickel-plated Colt sporting ivory grips strapped around his waist. He looked more like a gambler than any accountant Fargo had ever seen.

The second man wore shabby old buckskins. He had a shock of red hair and a square red beard which he constantly stroked. A bowie knife hung on his right hip, a Remington on his left.

Over by the window stood the third associate, a lanky, hard-eyed cowboy in jeans and a flannel shirt. A coiled lariat adorned his shoulder. He had neither Colt nor knife.

Last of all, except for the huge black man, was a half-breed, part Shoshoni or Crow by the looks of him, who wore worn buckskins and had a butcher knife in a beaded sheath on his right thigh. His dark eyes had been fixed on Fargo from the moment Fargo entered the room.

Fargo twisted and saw the black man standing relaxed over by the door. The man's build brought to mind that of a blacksmith, but it could just be that the black man had been born with more muscles than most men had hairs.

The five made for a strange assortment, Fargo mused. A gambler, a cowboy, a mountain man, a breed, and a blacksmith. It was plain that Morgan had hired them since arriving in Denver, since it was unlikely any of them came from anywhere east of the Mississippi. Why did a rich importer need the services of men like these? Fargo asked himself.

Suddenly Fargo became aware that Morgan had addressed him. He blinked and looked up. "What was that?"

"I asked whether you are a deputy."

Marshal Fedder answered first. "No. He's the one who was

assaulted by the owlhoot I'm hunting. I brought him along to point the man out to me in case we run into him."

Morgan had clipped the end of the cigar and was about to light it. He paused to inquire, "What might your name be, if I'm not prying?"

Fargo told him. Doing so had an odd effect on the mountain man, who stiffened, and the breed, who started to reach for the butcher knife but caught himself.

The lawman stood and smiled broadly. "Well, I reckon I won't take up any more of your time, Mr. Morgan. I thank you for being so helpful. If you should see the mangy wolf I'm after, I'd be obliged if you would contact my office."

"Most certainly, Marshal. I pride myself on my sense of civic duty."

Fargo went out last, without a backward glance, but had the distinct feeling that all eyes were on him. It made his skin crawl, reminding him of the time he accidentally found himself in a den of rattlesnakes high up in the Rockies. Something told him that the men in that room were every bit as deadly as those reptiles.

Fedder stayed silent until they were outdoors. "Well, what did you think?"

"There's more to Frederick Morgan than he lets on," Fargo said. "If I had to bet, I'd wager he knows more about the gunman than he admitted. But I have no idea what he's up to."

"Me, neither," Fedder said, rubbing his chin. "But I do know that you'd best watch your backside from here on out. Morgan would make a powerful enemy, and I'd swear that he was eyeing you just like a hungry wolf eyes a lost lamb." He paused. "One more thing. Did you recognize any of those so-called associates of his?"

"No"

"I did. That breed goes by the name of Charley Crow. He's part Crow and lived with the tribe for a spell, before they kicked him out for being too damn vicious. They say he likes to kill things just to see them squirm and bleed."

"I'll keep that in mind," Fargo said.

"Also keep in mind that the gent in the gray suit is a gambler with the handle of Pony Deal. He's lightning fast with that custom-made pistol of his, and when he's having a string of bad luck at cards he hires his gun out to the highest bidder. He has six notches to his credit, all supposedly in self-defense so there was nothing that could be pinned on him."

"What about the others?"

Marshal Fedder craned his neck to stare at Morgan's window. "The cowboy and the black man ring no bells, but that fellow with the red beard might be Eric Graven. He lives way up in the mountains and only comes down when someone needs a first-rate tracker. Word is he's one of the best. Maybe as good as you are."

Fargo digested the news with his brow knit. His hunch had proven right and it did not bode well for him. He'd gone up against more than his share of hard cases in his time, but the pack of killers Morgan had assembled made for a stacked deck few men could beat. He heard the marshal mutter and turned.

"Makes me wonder."

"What does?" Fargo prompted.

"About our friend in the floppy hat. I've heard that Pony Deal has a cousin named Dixie. The two stick closer together than two strands of binder twine. It could be that he's tied up in all this somehow." Fedder shook his head and patted Fargo on the shoulder. "Listen, son. I've got work to do. From here on, you're on your own. If I can help in any way, though, feel free to give a holler."

Fargo watched his lone ally amble off, then turned on his boot heel and headed west along Broadway. Plenty of pedestrians were abroad and the street was jammed with horses, wagons, and buggies. Dust choked the air, mingled with lusty curses that rose above the hubbub of voices and the racket raised by horses, mules, and dogs. The chaotic scene was a prime example of why Fargo liked the wide open spaces more than crowded cities.

Fargo walked slowly, as if deep in thought. Several times he stopped and admired articles for sale in store windows. He had gone seven blocks when he came to a mercantile with a gun display. A new Winchester was for sale, along with a matched set of Smith and Wessons and an old Hawken in remarkable condition. He studied each, then pulled out his Colt and hefted it, as if he were debating whether to trade it in on a new gun.

Finally Fargo twirled the pistol into its holster and turned to go. His eyes darted to the window, and there, reflected in the glass, was confirmation of a fact he had known since leaving the Summit House. He was being followed by the very worst of Morgan's bunch.

It was the breed.

4

Fargo pretended to wander aimlessly for the next quarter of an hour to give the impression he was taking in the sights Denver had to offer. All the while he was heading in the general direction of Cherry Creek.

The town fathers had seen fit to prevent construction for about a hundred yards on either side of the narrow waterway. The result was a lush belt of vegetation cutting through the very heart of Denver, a peaceful setting where families came to picnic and lovers to take a stroll.

Fargo remembered it well from a previous visit. He knew there were trails winding all through the trees and thickets, that in some places it was a virtual maze. At night decent people shunned Cherry Creek because of all the robbers, and worse, who lurked in the shadows, waiting to pounce on unwary innocents. It was made to order for what Fargo had in mind. He couldn't very well lead the breed back to the boardinghouse and put the lives of Melanie and Miss Dunn in jeopardy.

Soon the tops of cottonwoods and willows appeared above buildings to his right. Fargo walked another block and turned onto a narrow dirt trail. It was comforting to have walls of foliage close in on either side. He was in his element now and could confront Charley Crow on his own terms.

Fargo walked slowly along, as if he didn't have a care in the world, until he went around the first bend. Then he broke into a run and passed a couple watching the antics of a magpie. At the next junction he bore to the left onto another trail. Stopping, he crouched and peered through the brush at the bend.

Seconds later Charley Crow appeared, slinking along like a mountain lion on the prowl, one hand on the hilt of his butcher knife. The couple watching the magpie saw him and promptly moved on.

Rising and taking a step back, Fargo deliberately broke a slender branch on a bush bordering the trail. It would be enough of a clue for the breed. Hurrying along, he jogged for several minutes, winding steadily deeper into the belt of green, ever nearer to the creek, and ever farther from commonly used trails. He needed an isolated spot.

At length Fargo came on a site that suited him. It was less than ten feet from the edge of the gurgling water. On the right lay a fallen tree, the log as high as his waist. On the left grew thin grass just as high. He turned toward the log and took two steps, planting his boots firmly and heavily to be sure the prints were distinct. Then, exercising care, he retraced his steps by walking backward, placing his boots in the footprints already made.

From the middle of the trail, Fargo vaulted rearward into the high grass. He crouched, adjusted the stems so that it appeared the grass had not been disturbed, and flattened down. Drawing the Colt, he waited.

It was important that Fargo not move a muscle. A good woodsman learned to train himself to react to any motion, no matter how slight. A man like Charley Crow could detect the flicker of a fly's wings at twenty feet.

So Fargo held himself as still as the log on the other side of the trail. He didn't bat an eyelash when a yellow butterfly fluttered by, passing within an inch of his eyes. Nor did he move when a large bee decided he was worth a close scrutiny and nearly landed on his nose.

Then Fargo heard a very unique rustling sound, the sibilant scraping of scales across the ground, the sound that only a roaming snake could make. He knew the serpent was to his right and coming closer every second. He fought the urge to whip around—or to simply turn his head.

It might be a rattler, but the odds were slim. Rattlesnakes liked to hunt at night. And, too, the good people of Denver had a nasty habit of smashing any rattler they saw to a pulp.

Soon Fargo sensed the snake was right beside him. Something brushed his arm, drawing closer to his face. He swiveled his eyes and saw the creature's head appear, its red tongue darting out as it tested the air. The head was a light shade of brown with traces of green, and black markings. By the shape, it was obvious the snake wasn't a viper, and Fargo breathed easier.

The serpent slid into view, heading for the trail. Fargo recognized a wandering garter snake, as folks called them, perhaps the single most friendly snake in all the West. Even when provoked, they rarely bit, and they were so easily handled they made excellent pets for children.

Fargo watched the reptile glide from the grass onto the trail. Suddenly, from out of nowhere, a moccasin-covered foot slammed down onto the garter snake behind its head, pinning it in place. A gleaming blade slashed once, ripping the snake open from near the foot to the tip of its tail. Then the foot was withdrawn.

It was uncanny. Fargo hadn't heard any noise, hadn't registered the slightest movement, yet there stood the breed, bloody butcher knife dripping onto the trail. Charley Crow stood and observed the garter's death throes, the corners of his thin lips curled upward.

The snake thrashed and writhed, curling and uncurling until, tongue protruding, it went rigid and lay still.

Charley Crow bent and touched the tip of his knife to its head. For no apparent reason he dug the steel into the creature's brain and twisted.

Fargo was only three yards away. He could have shot the man dead, but he had other plans. It was important that he get answers, and the breed was going to supply them. He saw Charley Crow wipe the blade clean on the grass and shift to study his tracks. The killer's gaze drifted to the log.

As silently as a stalking lynx, Charley Crow slid toward the downed tree. He held the knife loosely at his side, ready for instant use.

Thinking that he had the man dead to rights, Fargo grinned and quietly pushed to his knees. He leveled the Colt, then opened his mouth to say, *Hold it right there, mister*. They were words he never uttered. For at the very moment he aimed the pistol, the breed sprang into action.

Charley Crow whirled and threw the butcher knife with practiced precision. No sooner did the hilt leave his fingers than he whirled again and leaped clear over the log. It was all done so swiftly that anyone who blinked would have missed it.

Fargo had no such luxury. He reacted in sheer reflex, diving to the left. The glistening blade streaked past his head, so close the air fanned his ear. Heaving off the ground, he darted to the log, the Colt at arm's length, the hammer cocked. He thought the breed would spring out at him, but when he reached the tree, Charley Crow was gone.

Turning left and right, Fargo scoured the strip of woodland. He knew the breed had to be close by somewhere, watching, yet try as he might, Fargo couldn't spot him. He moved to the middle of the trail and rotated three hundred and sixty degrees. Nothing.

During his travels Fargo had met many men, whites and Indians alike, whose woodlore was exceptional. But he couldn't recall a single one who rivaled the breed. Charley Crow was more Apache than Crow, a virtual ghost on two legs, and an extremely deadly man to have for an enemy.

Fargo's plan had backfired. Since he wasn't going to have his questions answered, he thought it best to get out of there. The breed might have another knife or a gun, and Fargo was the proverbial sitting duck.

His eyes constantly sweeping the foliage, Fargo took a bold gamble. It was always best to do the unexpected when one's life was at stake. So rather than go back the way he had come, which was the very thing Charley Crow no doubt expected, he dashed to Cherry Creek and quickly forded it. The shallow water came no higher than his ankles.

Once on the far bank, Fargo again scanned the vegetation flanking the creek. He thought he glimpsed a cruel face sneering at him, but when he focused on the spot, the face was gone.

Since there was no trail on this side, Fargo plunged into the brush and covered a full fifty yards before he halted to listen and study his back trail. He let five minutes go by. Assured the breed had elected not to follow, he went on to a trail and took it to a busy street. Here he stood under the overhang of a general store and watched the trees for another ten minutes. Many people went into and came out of the woods, but not one was Charley Crow.

Fargo counted himself lucky. He had temporarily given the murderous breed the slip. From there on out, however, he couldn't relax his vigilance for a minute. Sooner or later Charley Crow would show up, and the first inkling Fargo might have would be a burning sensation as cold steel sank deep into his flesh.

Blending with the pedestrians, Fargo hastened to the boardinghouse. All seemed tranquil as he approached, but he took no chances. He kept his back to the wall when he entered and went up the steps as if treading on eggshells. He planned to pack up his gear and go stay somewhere else.

At the top of the stairs, Fargo halted. His door stood ajar and he clearly recollected closing it. The landlady might have had cause to go in his room and left it open, but he'd be foolish to take that for granted.

Drawing the Colt, Fargo tiptoed to the jamb, moving his legs slowly enough so that his spurs wouldn't jingle. He heard a sigh, then the creak of a bedspring. Coiling his legs, he pushed the door wide and leaped into the room.

Melanie Landers snapped bolt upright in the bed and covered her mouth with a hand to stifle a scream. When she saw who it was, she relaxed and smiled. "It's you. For a second there I thought that terrible man had returned."

"What are you doing here?" Fargo asked as he replaced the six-shooter. "Miss Dunn will throw a hissy fit if she catches you in my room."

"Erica went to visit her sister on the other side of town and won't be back until around sunset," Melanie divulged. "She was kind enough to tell me that I could stay as long as I wanted. Once you get to know her, you learn that deep down she's a gem of a person."

"How are you feeling?" Fargo said. Stepping to the bed, he sat on the edge. Her face bore plenty of bruises, but her skin had a healthy glow and her lovely eyes sparkled with vitality.

"Much, much better, thank you. I just woke up a short while ago on the settee and came to see if you had shown up. I was worried."

"Where's that store clerk, Metz?"

"At work . . . where else?" Melanie stretched out on the pillow and languidly elevated her smooth arms, her bosom rising like a pair of inflating balloons. Her cherry lips formed an impish grin. She delicately traced their outline with the pink tip of her tongue, then remarked, "I've had more sleep than I need, I've helped myself to porridge and toast, and now all it would take to make the day perfect is a little loving."

"What if the landlady or Metz come back early?"

"So?" Melanie said. "I didn't take you for a fretter over trifles." She slid a shapely leg toward him. Her shoes were off, her dainty painted toes pale in the subdued light. Her big toe ran along his leg to the junction of his thighs. "Besides, which would you rather do, big man? Worry, or take up where we left off last night?"

"Need you ask?" Fargo unbuckled the gun belt and lowered it to the floor. He had the foresight to strip off his boots, too. A set of spurs could wreak havoc with quilts and bedsheets. Easing onto the bed next to her, he pressed his body flush against her warm form and gently touched one of her many black-and-blue marks. "What about those? I squeeze too hard or rub the wrong spot and you'll be in pain."

"If I don't care, why should you?"

Long ago Fargo had learned there was no arguing with feminine logic. It was her body. If that was the way she wanted it, fine by him.

"I want to thank you for saving me from that smelly son of a bitch," Melanie mentioned, while shifting so they were face to face.

"Smelly?" Fargo said.

"That man must never take a bath. I swear, I've smelled buffalo hunters who were more fragrant than he was."

Which was saying a lot. Buffalo hunters were notorious for reeking to high heaven. They spent their days knee-deep in guts and gore and blood, their nights drinking and whoring. Other than when they washed their hands to eat, water never touched their bodies. Some became so rank it was impossible to stand next to them and take a breath—unless you were another buffalo hunter.

Fargo filed the information away for future use and pressed his mouth to hers. Melanie had full, soft lips, the kind a man never tired of kissing or sucking on. She worked them against his, enticing him with their sweet taste. When he parted his lips, her silken tongue slid into his mouth and entwined with his.

Melanie was not one to lie still and let the man have all the fun. She roved her hands over Fargo's iron frame, savoring the feel of every muscle. She especially liked to rub his flat stomach, so unlike the flabby paunches of most men she had known.

For his part, Fargo was intent on her breasts. He plucked her buttons loose one by one, exposing her undergarments. These had to be loosened as well before the glorious prizes he sought popped free, the nipples already hardening with desire. Lowering his mouth to one, he sucked lightly, as a child might suck a lollipop. Some women liked to be squeezed so hard that they screamed, but he sensed Melanie wasn't one of them. She preferred the soft, tender treatment, which suited him just fine.

Fargo lathered first one heaving globe, then the other. Melanie contented herself with running her fingers through his hair and digging her nails into his shoulders every so often. Her legs swayed invitingly against him, her dress sliding practically to her hips, revealing an eyeful.

After a while Fargo drew back and quickly stripped her naked. She helped, the supple movements of her sleek body enough to drive him giddy with lust. She was exquisite living marble, highlighted by her pink nipples and the light thatch where her legs met. He took her breasts in his hands and massaged them with ever increasing urgency.

"This feels so wonderful," Melanie cooed. "I'd like to catch the rat who spoiled it for us last night and deprive him of his family jewels."

Fargo kissed her, her lips melting against his, her tongue a fiery sword that sent passion blazing through him. Some women were exceptional at kissing. Others seemed to think that all they had to do was pucker and close their eyes and the man would do all the rest. Thankfully, Melanie like to give as good as she got. Their kisses were liquid lava.

It was a while before Fargo allowed a hand to roam to her navel, and below. He ran a palm across her quivering belly to her thighs. She automatically parted her legs to grant him access to her core, but he was not about to get ahead of himself.

47

Life was meant to be savored, not experienced in greedy gulps.

"Mmmmmm," Melanie said. "I knew this would make me feel a lot better."

Fargo stroked her rippling tummy, stroked the sheer skin on her upper legs, then delved lower. She wriggled her bottom and pushed her nether mound against his arm. The back of his hand brushed her moist slit, eliciting heavy pants of excitement.

"I can hardly wait to have you inside of me," Melanie said huskily.

But Fargo put it off for a while longer, using his hands alone to arouse her to a fever pitch. She was clinging to him in wanton abandon when he finally slid a finger into her crack. The result was the same as if a bolt of lightning had struck her out of the blue.

Melanie arched her spine and gyrated her delightful posterior, her eyelids hooded, her breaths coming in ragged gasps of ardent pleasure. She raked his neck with her nails, then reached down to grasp his manhood.

"What are you waiting for, handsome? Do me."

"Be patient," Fargo growled, commencing a slow in-and-out motion with his finger, simulating the higher pleasure yet to come. She ground into him, groaning to the tempo of her sensual movements. The faster he went, the faster she did. Her mouth was parted in a delicious oval. Her breasts shook with every thrust, the nipples bobbing like miniature apples.

Fargo fastened his lips onto a breast and gave her double the joy. She couldn't get enough. Bucking against him as if she were a bronco trying to throw him off, she somehow contrived to hold his finger deep within her all the while.

His organ had long since become as hard as a rock. He was as ready as he would ever be.

Pushing her bent legs wide, Fargo revealed the slick petals of her inner flower. Parting them, he aligned himself just right, and then, when her breath caught in her throat in hungry anticipation, he lanced into her like a medieval knight at a joust. She came up off the bed as if trying to take wing, a squeal of raw animal emotion rising to the ceiling. His manhood was buried. Her pulsing body moved as if it had a mind of its own.

Fargo paced himself to prolong the inevitable. The bed creaked and squeaked under them, bouncing louder and louder as their urgency increased. In the back of Fargo's mind it occurred to him that if anyone else entered the house, the cause of the thumping would be obvious. But he shut the thought out and kept on pounding into Melanie, driving into her with a vengeance, his legs pumping like twin pump handles, the veins on his temples bulging.

Melanie cooed and groaned and lost herself in the joy of the moment. She caressed his back, his legs, and his chest. She reached down to cup his balls, which sent a tingle shooting up his back.

The bed moved, sliding out from the corner toward the center of the floor. The headboard swayed as if on the verge of collapse. Fargo didn't care. He was close to the brink and knew that she was also. Gripping her hips, he stroked with renewed vigor, hoping to send her over the edge. Her staying power was the equal of his, though, and they continued their rhythmic rocking for a full five minutes more.

The first sign of the impending climax came when Melanie cried out and then shook as if suddenly cold. She exploded, throwing herself upward as if to impale herself on his pole, her mouth devouring his.

Fargo tried to hold back a little longer but his body was not to be denied. His explosion matched hers. The bedroom spun before his eyes and the bed seemed to float up off the floor. He pumped and pumped, draining himself dry. When at last he was totally spent, he collapsed on top of her sweating figure, his head cushioned by her yielding breasts.

"Lordy, that was marvelous," Melanie whispered. She tugged at his soaked hair, then ran a finger along the outer edge of his ear. "If I'd known it was going to be this fine, I would have done it last night no matter how I felt at the time."

Peaceful minutes passed. Fargo relished the serenity. He heard the beat of her heart slow from a wild pounding to a regular rate. Her skin was deliciously cool against his, and he was reluctant to get up and do what he had to do.

Soon Fargo dozed off. He had no idea how long he slept, but suddenly he was wide awake, certain that a noise had brought him around. Ears straining, he rose on an elbow. Melanie was still sound asleep, her lower lip fluttering as she breathed. After listening a while, he figured that he had been mistaken and went to lower his head.

A floorboard creaked somewhere in the boardinghouse.

Instantly Fargo slid silently off the bed and hiked his pants. Picking up his gun belt, he drew the Colt and padded in his stocking feet to the door, which he had made the mistake of leaving wide open.

Fargo moved to the landing. Faint footsteps sounded from the vicinity of the downstairs sitting room—stealthy footsteps, unlike those the landlady would make, or Metz, for that matter. Someone was in the house who had no business being there.

His back to the wall, Fargo descended. Through the rails of the banister, he could see part of the main corridor and the doorway to the sitting room. A shadow flicked across it.

Fargo dropped into a crouch at the foot of the stairs and worked his way around to within a stride of the doorway. He saw the shadow again. Holding the six-shooter close to his chest, he girded himself, then bounded into the room, ready for anything. Only no one was there.

Mystified, Fargo scoured the room closely. It was impossible for anyone to have left without him seeing them, unless they went out one of the windows. He glanced at the nearest window, then understood.

Perched on an oak tree outside were a number of sparrows. They were flitting back and forth from branch to branch in a playful frolic. And the sun, streaming in through the window from above and behind them, cast their shadowed movements on the floor and the doorway.

But what about the creaking floorboard and the footsteps he thought he had heard? Fargo wondered. It was a known fact that old houses were forever making noise. The explanation might be that simple, yet his gut feeling was that he should check further.

Fargo moved out into the hall and headed for the far end of

the house, where Miss Dunn had her own bedroom. He saw the kitchen ahead. Before reaching it he must pass a junction where another hall branched off. A shadow took shape on the floor there, and this time it wasn't the shadow of a bird. It was a person, slowly approaching the main corridor. Fargo stopped and touched his finger to the trigger of his Colt.

Around the corner walked Felicia Taugner.

5

The petite schoolmarm was the very last person Fargo expected to see. She blinked at the sight of his Colt and started to back against the wall in apparent fear for her life. Fargo quickly lowered the pistol and shoved it in his holster. With her being from the East, it was doubtful she had ever been around guns much. He didn't want to scare the living daylights out of her.

"My word!" she exclaimed. "You gave me a horrible fright. Do you always go around pointing firearms at visitors?"

"You're a fine one to talk," Fargo grumbled. "Do you always go around walking into the homes of people you don't know without bothering to knock?"

"For your information, I did rap on the door," Felicia said. "No one answered. Perhaps I shouldn't have taken it on myself to walk in unannounced, but I was hoping to learn where I could find you."

Fargo began tucking in his shirt. "How did you know I was staying here? I don't recall telling you."

"Marshal Fedder was kind enough to inform me when I stopped by his office a short while ago. I hope you won't mind my showing up in this fashion. It's extremely important that we talk again."

"After you," Fargo said, indicating the sitting room. "We might as well make ourselves comfortable."

Her fingers nervously toying with a button, the schoolmarm moved gingerly past him and went in. She took a seat on the settee without being told and carefully smoothed her dress. "I apologize for waking you from your nap. I didn't think you would be sleeping at this time of the day."

"Don't fret yourself," Fargo said, not about to tell her the real reason he had been in bed.

Felicia sat back, her legs pressed tight together in a ladylike manner. "I was wondering if you had made up your mind yet about acting as our guide."

"I only saw you this morning. I need more time to think the offer over," Fargo reminded her, while strapping on his gun belt. "Besides, you told me that the other two teachers won't arrive in Denver for another two or three days."

"I was wrong," Felicia said. "I've received word that both of them will be on the evening stage. Since the fine people of Banner, Wyarno, and Bighorn are eagerly waiting for us to reach their settlements, I though it prudent for us to leave as soon as practical."

"How soon?" Fargo asked.

"Tomorrow morning."

Fargo had been about to sit down, but he stayed on his feet. "That's too soon, even if I agreed to take you."

"Find us someone else, then," Felicia said. "Anyone will do."

Fargo frowned. The woman had no idea what she was asking. Locating someone else on such short notice would be hard enough. Locating someone she could trust to get her to the settlements would be even harder. There were plenty of men who'd leap at the chance to earn the money but who had never been more than ten miles north of Denver. They'd only wind up getting her party lost or killed.

"I can tell you're unhappy. Please explain why."

Mincing no words, Fargo did, concluding with, "There's another reason that leaving tomorrow is out of the question. You'll need supplies and decent pack animals, which don't grow on trees. It will take at least a day to organize everything."

"Oh, dear," Felicia said. "I was so anxious to leave, too." She fidgeted, her legs swaying slightly. An ordinary enough movement, yet somehow it was intensely stimulating.

Fargo reminded himself that he really must try to keep his mind on the matter at hand. "The day after tomorrow is the best I could do."

The schoolmarm brightened, showing even, white teeth. "You'll do it, then? Oh, how marvelous!"

"Hold on," Fargo said testily. "I haven't made any promises yet. I need to think some more."

Felicia gave her right foot a tiny stamp. "Honestly, I had no idea frontiersmen enjoy such an intellectual bent. What is there to think about? It's either yes, you will, or no, you won't. I do so dislike being kept in suspense this way."

A sharp reply was on the tip of Fargo's tongue. He had been as polite as a church deacon to her and as honest as the day was long. It got his goat that she saw fit to treat him as if he were her worst enemy when all he was trying to do was help her out the best he could. But as he went to vent his spleen, into the room waltzed Melanie Landers.

Miss Felicia Taugner gawked. As well the teacher might, considering that Melanie was only partially dressed. She had put the dress on but not bothered to fasten more than a button or two. As a result, she was showing more cleavage than would have been legal out on the street. Melanie also wore a contented smirk as she sashayed in, and gave Fargo a smile that could melt ice at twenty paces.

"So there you are, handsome. I woke up and wanted someone to cuddle with, but you were gone."

"I have company," Fargo said crustily.

Melanie gave Felicia an amused glance. "So you do. Where did you find her? If she was any stiffer, I swear she'd be a board."

The schoolmarm turned an indignant red. Fargo held a laugh in and tried to soothe her by saying, "Don't mind my friend. She's more outspoken than most."

"The way she spills out of her clothes, I'm not the least bit surprised," Felicia said.

Melanie placed her hands on her hips. "Just what in the hell is that supposed to mean, missy? Don't you ever lounge about your house in whatever feels comfortable?" She paused. "No, I imagine you don't. You strike me as the type who irons her underwear."

"Now, see here!" Felicia bristled, coming off the settee. "I won't tolerate being insulted by a hussy like you. You should work on your manners when you're not so busy lounging about."

Fargo thought Melanie was going to tear into the school-marm. It tickled him that the two had come so close to blows within sixty seconds of meeting one another. And women liked to claim that men were hotheaded! He rose and stepped between them. "All right, ladies. That's enough. Melanie, go back upstairs and I'll be with you in a bit."

The dove pouted but complied. She couldn't resist a last taunt, though. "A pleasure making your acquaintance, dear," she told Felicia, speaking with perfect diction, as if she were a guest at an upper-crust tea party. Then she reverted to more earthy speech. "Look me up at the Bull's Head if you ever decide to start living a life like the rest of us poor unwashed trash."

Fire danced in Felicia's eyes but she offered no response. After Melanie had gone, she turned to Fargo and coughed. "I don't know as I can speak highly of your choice in friends."

Fargo shrugged. "We have a saying out here, Miss Taugner. Secondhand gold and silver is as good as new. It applies to people, too."

"Ah. You're accusing me of being too quick to judge her."

"I'm not accusing you of anything," Fargo said. "I'm simply telling you how things are." He gestured at the hall. "Now, why don't you run along and I'll get back to you as soon as I can."

"If you insist," Felicia said, displeased. She took a few steps, then abruptly paused. "Perhaps you would see fit to do me a favor, Mr. Fargo."

"Depends on what it is."

"The Leavenworth and Pike's Peak Express is due in at six this evening. I would be ever so grateful if you would agree to meet me at the company office so I can introduce you to my associates."

"What for?" Fargo demanded, since the idea made no sense that he could see. He'd meet the other teachers soon enough, if he agreed to guide them.

"I'm afraid I'm not very adept at persuading people," Felicia said. "Perhaps if you were to talk to them, they might succeed where I've failed."

55

"It can wait—," Fargo began, but stopped when he saw the hurt and hint of desperation that lined her attractive features. He decided he might as well get it over with so she would stop pestering him. "You win, ma'am. I'll be there at six. But I'm warning you in advance that they won't be able to change my mind."

"You never know," Felicia said, suddenly lighthearted. She nodded and walked out.

Fargo moved to the hall to watch her. For so small a woman, she had as fine a figure as he had ever seen. It was too bad her heart was as cold as the snow crowning the Rockies. If she ever melted, she would give Melanie a run for her money. So to speak.

Chuckling, Fargo went up the stairs and nearly collided with the saloon girl, who was now fully presentable. She veered to the left to go around him. "Hold on," he said, taking her arm. "Where are you off to in such a hurry?"

"Someplace away from you," Melanie said, tugging loose. "I don't much like the fact that you didn't stand by me down there."

"What are you talking about?"

"You sent me away instead of her. And after the grand time we had together! Makes me wonder if there's a man anywhere worth a damn."

"You're not being fair," Fargo said, but his protest was wasted. She hastened to the screen door and slammed it behind her. He knew that her attitude shouldn't surprise him, but it did. Women, after all, could be just as contrary as men when they put their minds to it.

Fargo sighed and went into his room to pack up. He still didn't think it safe for him to remain at the boardinghouse. Charley Crow might show up at any time, and such a cold-blooded killer wouldn't hesitate to slay Miss Dunn or the other boarder if either accidentally got in his way.

It took but a few minutes to prepare his bedroll and tie his saddlebags. Throwing each over a shoulder, he picked up the Sharps and walked downstairs. Instead of going out the front, he turned and went the length of the corridor to the kitchen. A back door opened onto a small yard neatly decorated with colorful flowers.

Fargo hesitated just long enough to place several coins on the tabletop. Erica Dunn would know it was his way of saying thanks for the aggravation he had unwittingly caused.

Pushing the door wide, Fargo eased outside. A plank fence bordered the yard, preventing him from seeing whether anyone lurked nearby. He crossed to a gate, threw the bolt, and took a single step.

Without warning, a pistol materialized next to Fargo's head. The muzzle lightly tapped his temple and he heard the hammer being cocked. Since to make any move at all would result in his death, Fargo froze. He thought the breed had found him, but he was wrong.

From around the corner of the fence stepped the short man in the floppy hat and sheepskin coat. Two of his top teeth were missing, as his cocky grin revealed. He declared in a Southern drawl, "I hear tell you've been lookin' for me, mister. Well, here I am."

The man holding the gun moved into view. "He doesn't look any too happy to see you, Eric Graven said. Up close, the mountain man's red beard resembled a tangled thicket.

"That he doesn't," Dixie agreed. "And after all the trouble I went to in settin' up our surprise."

Fargo glanced in both directions, hoping someone might have noticed and would notify the marshal. The alley was empty save for them.

"He seems a mite worried to me," the killer in buckskins said. "Maybe he's afeared we'll blow his brains out right here and now."

Dixie snickered. "No such luck, mister. You have some questions to answer first." Leering, he plucked Fargo's Colt free and wedged it under his gun belt, then took the Sharps. "Now here's what we'll do. I want you to mosey on down to Hancock Street yonder and take a right. We'll be right behind you. If you get the notion to make a break for it, try to remember that one of us will put a bullet into you before you take two steps."

"In broad daylight?" Fargo said, stalling.

"We're being paid to do a job, mister, and it doesn't hardly matter whether we do it in the middle of the day or the middle of the night," Dixie said. "So get movin'."

Faced with no other choice, Fargo obeyed. "I'll say one thing for your boss, Morgan. The man has more sand than most."

Graven laughed. "This ornery bastard is trying to be clever, Dixie. He's trying to trick us into admitting we work for somebody named Morgan."

"Clever son of a gun, ain't he?" Dixie said, and prodded Fargo in the small of the back with the rifle. "Well, I have news for you, mister. We don't know anyone with that handle. We're doing this on our own."

"Sure you are," Fargo said. He winced when he was prodded again, much harder. They went past a half-dozen homes without seeing a soul. When they neared Hancock, Graven slipped his Remington into his holster, but kept his hand on the butt.

"To the right," Dixie reminded Fargo.

There were a few people on the side street, and only two saw fit to glance in Fargo's direction. To them, everything appeared normal. Fargo walked dozens of feet and came abreast of a vacant office building. The window bore a sign proclaiming it was for rent and the address of the owner."

"Here we are," Dixie announced. "Go on in."

The latch had been broken. All Fargo had to do was push and the door swung open on oiled hinges. He stepped into a small, empty room and was given a rough shove that sent him stumbling to its middle. Turning, he was careful to make no sudden moves. Both Graven and Dixie covered him.

"Let's get crackin'," the latter said. "I don't aim to spend all day at this." He wagged Fargo's Colt. "Drop the stuff, mister. You won't be havin' any need for it in a little while, anyway."

The bedroll and saddlebags hit the floorboards with dull thuds. Fargo had to buy time to think of a way to turn the tables, so he said, "What is this all about? Why did you jump me in my room last night?"

"We'll ask the questions," Dixie said, and took a step nearer. "Does she know?"

"Who? What?" Fargo responded. He was unprepared for the brutal blow delivered to his gut, as the gunman darted forward and rammed his own pistol into him. Fargo buckled. Pain shot from his hips to his toes, and for several seconds it was questionable whether he would hold down his last meal. On hands and knees, he looked up at his tormentor. "That was a mistake."

"You've got me tremblin' in my boots," Dixie said, grinning.

"Look, mister," Graven threw in. "We can do this the hard way, if you want, but you can spare yourself a lot of misery if you'll just answer us honestly. We know that she was looking all over Denver for you. How much has she told you? Are they in this together?"

Fargo knew they were referring to the schoolmarm, but the rest was a complete mystery. "I don't have any damn idea what you're talking about," he said.

Dixie took a step and kicked. Fargo tried to evade the boot, but it caught him flush in the ribs and added to the agony in his midsection.

"You're as stubborn as a jackass, ain't you?" the short gunman said. "We're going to get the truth out of you one way or another, so why not fess up and get it over with?"

"Go to hell," Fargo growled. He had taken all the punishment he was going to take. One way or another, he would pay the sawed-off runt back.

Graven moved to one side. "I reckon this varmint has to learn everything the hard way. Pound on him some more, Dixie Lee. Maybe that will loosen his fool tongue."

"I doubt it," Dixie said, elevating the Colt. "Hold still, now, mister. It'll just be worse for you if you don't."

Fargo braced his legs to leap. So intent were the two hired killers on him that when a fist pounded on the door, both jumped and spun.

"Skye? Are you all right?" Melanie Landers called out. "What's going on?"

"Damn!" the mountain man said. "Where'd she come from?"

In a fluid move, Fargo slammed into Dixie Lee's back. The half-pint hit the door with jarring force, even as Fargo whirled to meet Eric Graven's rush. The bearded man tried to brain Fargo instead of shooting. Fargo sidestepped the swing, grabbed Graven's arm as it flashed past, and heaved. The mountain man did a somersault and crashed onto his back, the gun flying from his nerveless fingers.

Fargo was aware that Dixie Lee had jerked the door open. He heard Melanie's piercing scream. But before he could go to her aid, Graven came up off the floor with that bowie knife cocked to slash and cut. Fargo skipped to the right and the blade missed him by a hair. He tried to seize Graven's wrist, but this time the mountain man was too fast for him.

A scuffle broke out in the doorway. From the street came shouts and the drum of running feet. Someone was coming to see what all the fuss was about. All Fargo had to do was stay alive a little longer.

Which was far easier said than done. Graven had spent years high up in the Rockies where cougars and grizzlies roamed. He had lived among the Indians. His wilderness skills were the equal of Fargo's. Using a knife and breathing were one and the same to him.

Fargo barely missed having his neck opened. He blocked a thrust at his groin, clutched Graven's wrist, and twisted, striving to make the man drop the bowie. Graven merely howled with rage and ripped his arm free.

"You'll die for that, bastard!"

This time the bowie speared at Fargo's chest. The razor edge nicked his buckskin shirt as he sprang out of its path. Fargo had a knife of his own but it was in his boot. If he tried to grab it, the mountain man would finish him off.

A shot rang out outside. Melanie screamed again.

Anxious to help her, dreading a slug in the back courtesy of Dixie Lee, Fargo became reckless. Instead of leaping backward when Graven stabbed once more, he slid in close and buried his fist in the man's abdomen.

Most men would have crumpled on the spot. Eric Graven was as hard as a rock. He shrugged off the punch and aimed a swift blow at Fargo's jugular. Fargo ducked, then threw himself at the mountain man's knife arm. Locking both hands on Graven's wrist, he tried to trip him, but Graven pranced to the rear, hauling Fargo with him. Struggling mightily, they passed through a door into a larger office. This one wasn't empty.

Fargo saw a desk behind the mountain man and drove forward. The killer smashed into the desktop, lost his balance, and toppled. Fargo tried to hold on and couldn't. He went to dart around the desk, but Graven regained his feet with remarkable speed and swung the bowie, holding Fargo at bay.

"Skye? Where are you?"

Melanie's yell relieved Fargo, since it proved she was still alive. Too occupied to reply, he feinted to the left, shifted, and dove over the desk, catching Graven in the chest. They landed side by side. Fargo rolled backward and heard the knife thunk into the floor inches from his head. He pushed upright, sliding the Arkansas toothpick from its ankle sheath.

But the mountain man was no longer in front of him. Graven had spun and dashed to a window. Arms over his face to protect his eyes, he plunged through the glass, which shattered into dozens of fragments and flying shards.

Fargo ran to the sill.

Graven was already up and fleeing down the alley. There was no trace of blood. By some miracle, he had not been cut. He glanced back once to shake his fist, his expression saying more than words ever could.

"There you are!"

Into the room ran Melanie. She stared out at the fleeing mountain man, then up at Fargo. "The other one cuffed me a few times, then ran off down the street when he saw people coming from all directions." She put her hand on his arm. "Are you hurt?"

"Only my pride," Fargo said, turning. He saw a fresh bruise on her cheek and shook his head. "Just what you needed. Another black-and-blue mark."

"I'm buying a derringer before this day is done. The next man who slaps me is in for a nasty surprise."

Taking her hand, Fargo walked to the outer office. Ten or eleven citizens were crowded outside. They all commenced asking questions at once, but fell quiet when Fargo held up an arm.

"Thank you for helping out. Everything is fine now. You can go on about your business."

"Shouldn't someone fetch the marshal?" one asked.

"I'm going straight to his office," Fargo disclosed. They slowly dispersed, whispering amongst themselves. He squeezed Melanie's hand and said, "I'm obliged. I owe you." Fargo touched her chin. "What were you doing here?"

"I came back to the boardinghouse to say I was sorry for acting like a ten-year-old," Melanie said. "You weren't there, though. I happened to look out the back window and saw you leave with those men. Something about it wasn't quite right, so I followed a long ways back. When you went into this place, I decided to find out what was going on." She gave him a searching look. "What *is* going on?"

Skye Fargo picked his hat up off the floor and wiped dust from the brim. "I wish to hell I knew," he said, and meant every word.

6

The Gold Nugget was, without exception, the finest place to eat in all of Denver. Its owner had spared no expense to attract those with money to burn, going so far as to import a chef all the way from fabled Delmonico's in New York City. The dishes this wizard whipped up were the talk of the town, thanks to a kitchen worker who had smuggled a menu out. It hadn't been long before the good people of Denver were all in a dither over the very idea of folks eating frog legs and fish eggs and such. The very thought made many feel ill.

Skye Fargo recalled these facts as he trailed Marshal Fedder into the lavish foyer. A man in a neatly pressed black suit barred their path, a fake smile plastered on his face.

"Excuse me, gentlemen, but there is a dress code at the Nugget. If you want to dine here, you'll need to go home and change first."

"Out of our way, pup," the lawman declared.

To Fargo's surprise, the man made no attempt to obey.

"I'm sorry, sir, but part of my job is to see to it that no one gets in unless they are properly attired. You and your friend in buckskins will have to leave."

Marshal Fedder bristled. "Like hell we will." He shifted so the glow from a nearby lamp caught him squarely, and tapped his tin star. "This is my job, mister. And this badge gives me the right to go anywhere I want, any damn time I please. So get out of our way, or I'll have you thrown in jail until the cows come home."

The man blinked a few times, then said, "Sorry, Marshal. I didn't notice. The lighting in here isn't as bright as it could be."

"Probably so your customers won't see those frog legs hopping around on their plates," Fedder declared. He brushed on past and stalked into the main dining area.

Fargo spied Frederick Morgan right away. The rich importer sat at a large polished table in the center, attended by three waiters who hovered over him like hummingbirds over a bowl of sugar water. Morgan dined alone. He glanced up as they approached and adjusted the white napkin tucked under the neck of his shirt.

"Mr. Fargo. And the marshal. To what do I owe the pleasure, gentlemen?"

"Spare me the bull," Fedder said. "You know damn well why we're here. Not an hour ago one of your so-called associates and another coyote by the name of Dixie Lee tried to kill Fargo. Don't try to deny it, because I've corralled witnesses." Fedder looked around. "Where are those men of yours? I want to get my hands on that mountain man, Graven."

Morgan smiled thinly. "Mr. Graven is no longer in my employ."

"What?"

"I assure you, it's true. I dismissed him shortly after your visit this morning." Morgan picked up a glass of red wine and swirled the contents. "Originally, I planned to do some hunting up in the mountains and to use Mr. Graven as my guide. But now it turns out I won't be in Denver as long as I thought I might, so the hunting trip is off."

Fargo simply stared. He knew it was a barefaced lie, but he lacked proof. Morgan must have guessed they would pay him a visit and sent Graven into hiding. The man was deviously clever. Fargo made a mental note to never underestimate him again.

"You must be disappointed," Fedder said dryly. "But what about Pony Deal? Where's he?"

"Why do you want him, if I might ask?"

"Because Dixie Lee is his pard. I figure Pony will know where to find him."

"Unfortunately, I sent Mr. Deal and Mr. Crow south on an important errand for me. They should be back in four or five days," Morgan said.

The lawman didn't hide his anger well. "South where?"

"I don't see where that is any of your business, since their errand is highly personal," Morgan answered. "But if you want to press the issue, I'm sure my lawyers will be more than happy to sit down with you and discuss it."

Fargo knew when they were licked, and so did the marshal.

"Never mind," Fedder said. "I'd rather tangle with a bunch of stampeding buffalo than a bunch of uppity law wranglers." He nudged Fargo. "Let's go before I see someone eating fish eggs. I don't want my breakfast coming back up on me."

For two bits Fargo would have walked over and slugged Morgan in the mouth. If they had been out in the wild, it would have been child's play for him to pry the truth from Morgan, one way or another. But when in a town or city, he had to obey the law just like anyone else or wind up behind bars, and if there was one thing Fargo hated more than anything, it was being penned up against his will. So he contented himself with glaring at Morgan and then walked from the restaurant.

The lawman turned to say something, but hesitated, his gaze going over Fargo's shoulder. Fargo turned and saw a deputy running toward them.

"It's Bonham," Fedder said. "You met him at my office earlier."

The young deputy drew up, winded. "Marshal, you've got to come, quick. Someone found a body." He glanced sadly at Fargo, then averted his eyes. "I reckon you'll want to come, too, mister. This might concern you."

A bad feeling came over Fargo, a feeling that grew worse and worse as they hurried along Denver's dusty streets to the very saloon where he had won at stud poker the night before. A crowd had gathered at the mouth of an alley east of the building. The curious parted for the lawmen, and Fargo dogged their heels into the shadows.

Another deputy and a man holding a doctor's black bag stood beside a prone figure shrouded with a green blanket.

"She was strangled, Ed," the sawbones addressed Marshal Fedder. "It's the worst I've ever seen. Whoever did it has to be as strong as an ox."

Fargo knew who it was even before the young deputy stooped to lift the blanket high enough for them to see. The last time he had seen her had been at the marshal's office, shortly before leaving to find Morgan. She'd promised to meet him at the boardinghouse later, but first she had to tell her boss that she was taking the night off so he could get another woman to fill in for her at the saloon.

Melanie's features were strangely peaceful considering how she had met her end. Her neck had been squeezed to a pulp by steely fingers, leaving great grooves in her soft flesh. She had struggled fiercely, as blood and skin under her nails showed. Her dress had been badly torn.

Skye Fargo went all cold inside. Sinking to one knee, he examined her right hand, studying her long fingernails.

"Was she—," Marshal Fedder started to ask, without finishing the question.

"I won't know for sure until I complete the postmortem exam," the doctor said, "but if you want my opinion, the answer is no. Whoever did this was only interested in killing her, nothing else."

Fargo gently lowered Melanie's arm, stood, and moved to one side to get his surging emotions under control. He felt as if her death was partly his fault, which was nonsense since he'd had no way of knowing that she would be targeted. What had she done, other than unwittingly save his hide? he asked himself. Was that why they killed her? To punish her for meddling? It made him so mad, his head swam.

A hand fell on Fargo's shoulder. "I'm sorry, son. I truly am. I know you were fond of that filly."

"What will you do?" Fargo asked, his voice husky with strain.

"Ask around. Try to rustle up a witness or two."

"And if you can't?" Fargo inquired, turning.

Marshal Fedder was the picture of dejection. "You know the answer to that one. No matter what I might *like* to do, my hands are tied by the law I'm sworn to uphold. I can't do anything unless I have proof." He paused, looked around to verify no one was listening, then added, "I'll tell you this, though, and it's strictly between us." Fedder nodded at the corpse. "If that was my friend lying there, I'd move heaven and hell, if need be. Those sons of bitches can't go unpunished. It just wouldn't be right."

The lawman went over to the doctor, leaving Fargo to walk

from the alley alone. Something in his eyes caused everyone in his path to move quickly out of his way.

Fargo walked for hours. He knew that Fedder was right, knew exactly what he had to do. So it was that shortly before six o'clock that evening he arrived at the stage station and found Felicia Taugner awaiting him out front. She acted amazed.

"I can't believe you actually came! Thank you! Once you've met the other teachers, I'm positive you'll agree to take us to the settlements." The schoolmarm paused, studying him. "Are you all right? You appear terribly upset."

Taking a deep breath, Fargo willed the tension from his mind and body and hooked his thumbs in his gun belt. "I'm fine," he lied. "And you'll be happy to hear that your friends won't need to persuade me. I'll guide you north for the price you set."

Felicia clapped her hands in delight. "Really and truly? Oh, this is wonderful beyond words! How soon can we leave?"

"Tomorrow at noon."

"That soon?" Felicia said. "What about the pack animals and supplies? I thought you told me it would take a full day to obtain them."

"I know a few people," Fargo said. "If I push it, we can be ready to go about midday. The trip itself, if we ride hard and don't run into trouble, will take about two weeks."

The schoolmarm impulsively gripped Fargo's hand. "I can't express my gratitude enough. This means so much to me."

Just then a tremendous racket broke out at the end of the street, and moments later the stage swept into view, creaking and rattling noisily, the team sweaty from the long haul. The driver cracked his whip a few times to impress the onlookers.

In a swirling cloud of dust the stage slowed to a stop in front of the office. The manager and others were on hand to greet it, and for a minute hectic activity partially hid those who climbed down. Fargo saw a heavyset man in a cheap suit collect his bags and move off. Then a woman with a child. Finally another woman and a man appeared and gazed uncertainly around.

"That's them!" Felicia squealed, acting as giddy as a girl

meeting long-lost kin. "I recognize them from the descriptions they sent me."

One of the teachers fit Fargo's idea of how a teacher should look. It was the man, who was not much over five feet in height and had a face like a chipmunk's and wore spectacles. He also wore a seedy brown suit that had seen better days years ago. He took off his glasses to wipe them with a handkerchief while giving Denver a critical look down his angular nose.

The other teacher was another story. The woman was as different from prim Felicia Taugner as night from day. She had raven tresses that cascaded past her fine shoulders, and wore a dress that Melanie would have liked. Her green eyes were the kind that drove men wild. And her body drew masculine stares like honey drew bears.

Fargo stayed where he was as Felicia moved forward to greet the pair.

"Mr. Squib! Miss Langtree! Thank goodness you made it. I'm Felicia Taugner."

They shook hands. Felicia brought them over and made formal introductions. Ernest Squib had a limp, cold shake, and judging by his expression, he took an immediate dislike to Fargo. Which was only fair, since Fargo took an immediate dislike to him.

Elizabeth Langtree had hands as warm as embers from a fire. Her smile of greeting was sincere. And her voice resembled the purring of a great mountain cat. "I'm pleased to make you acquaintance, Mr. Fargo. I've never met an honest-to-goodness frontier scout before." Her hands lingered on his own. "I'm from Ohio, you see."

Just a few days earlier Fargo would have said or done something to let her know he was interested in her in more ways than one, but it was too soon after Melanie's death. The ghastly image of her crushed throat hovered before his mind's eye, kindling his simmering rage. "You've come a long way," was all he said.

"I've always wanted to see the West," Elizabeth remarked. "Who hasn't, after all the tales that are told about the glorious adventures one can have out here?"

"Sometimes those adventures can get you killed," Fargo noted.

Ernest Squib sniffed. "My sentiments exactly. Were it not for the fact I have not been employed in over two years and am desperate for work, I would have declined this job." He sniffed the dusty air, then coughed. "I do so hope this climate isn't bad for my health. I'm allergic to a few things, you see. Dust, grass, and animals make me so ill I can hardly stand it."

Fargo stared at the dozens of horses in the street, at the clouds of dust rising from their hooves, and, through a gap between the stage office and the next building, at the sea of waving grass beyond the town limits. "I'd say your health is in for a big change."

"I have great news," Felicia Taugner announced. "We can leave tomorrow by twelve o'clock. So I would suggest we all turn in early tonight to be well rested."

Squib nodded. "Sounds good to me. After being tossed around inside that awful coach for the better part of a week, I for one would love to stretch out on a bed again."

Elizabeth Langtree glanced at Fargo. "What about you? Are you turning in early, too? I was hoping to see some of the sights before we moved on."

Twice now the woman had come on to him, and Fargo didn't know what to make of it. She was a schoolmarm, and schoolmarms weren't supposed to do such things. He was keenly tempted to take her up on her not so subtle invitation, but he couldn't shake that picture of Melanie's body. And he couldn't ignore the danger to anyone with whom he associated. "I have other plans," he said curtly.

"Too bad," Miss Langtree said, and sighed. "Oh, well. What next, Miss Taugner?"

"We'll take your bags to the hotel and go out to eat," Felicia said. The newcomers moved to fetch their luggage and she moved closer to Fargo. "Where should we meet you tomorrow?"

"I'll be at the Imperial with all the horses and pack animals we should need about eleven," Fargo said. "Have them ready and waiting so we can load all your belongings and be on our way."

"Will do," Felicia pledged, and surprised him by clasping

his hands as Langtree had done. "Again, I can't thank you enough. With you to guide us, I'm certain everything will turn out all right."

Fargo didn't share her optimism. He said so long and headed for the marshal's office to claim his bedroll and saddlebags. Several blocks had fallen behind him when he had the same feeling he had experienced earlier that day, when Charley Crow stalked him. He was being followed again.

Slowing as he went around a corner, Fargo casually cast his eyes at the ranks of pedestrians lining the boardwalk. It was that time of the day when clerks and bankers and bakers headed home from a long day of work, when gamblers and doves and rowdies headed for their favorite haunts. The streets were packed. Trying to pick one person out of the throng was next to impossible.

Fargo hoped it was Charley Crow. He wanted dearly to pay Morgan back for Melanie's death, and the breed was high on his list of those who might have done the deed. Certainly Morgan hadn't strangled her himself. Frederick Morgan would never soil his hands doing his own dirty work.

Quickening his pace, Fargo went two more blocks. A crowd of noisy prospectors was in front of him, passing a bottle back and forth. He gathered that one of them had hit some color and they were celebrating.

As the prospectors came even with an alley, Fargo started to dart past them on the inside of the boardwalk. There was barely enough room for someone to squeeze by, which suited him just fine. He had timed his move so that he could duck into the alley with little risk of being spotted by the stalker.

Drawing his Colt, Fargo pressed his back to the left-hand wall and waited. Men and women streamed past, hardly any giving him so much as a glance. Then came someone he recognized, but it wasn't Charley Crow.

The desk clerk from the Imperial, where the schoolteachers were staying, was strolling along as if he didn't have a care in the world, munching from a sack of peanuts. He gave out a startled yelp when Fargo grasped his collar and hauled him into the alley.

"What the hell are you doing following me, Edwards?" Fargo demanded.

Edwards had his mouth ajar, half-eaten peanuts lying on his tongue. He swallowed, sputtered, then blurted, "I don't know what you mean, mister. I just got off work and was out for some exercise. How dare you lay your hand on me!"

Fargo took a menacing step. "Do you expect me to believe that you just happened by?"

The man stiffened. "I don't care what you believe. I have half a mind to notify the marshal."

It took all of Fargo's self-control to keep from bashing the clerk's face in. He knew in his bones that Edwards was lying. But he was at a loss to explain why the man should shadow him, and there was nothing he could do about it short of beating Edwards senseless. "I'll warn you only once," he declared. "If I catch you slinking after me again, you'll be sorry."

Holstering the Colt, Fargo merged with the flow on the boardwalk. The idea of leaving town the next day appealed to him greatly. He was sick to death of all the crowds and noise, sick to death of clerks and sidewalks and feeling as if he were adrift in a maze with no end in sight. He longed for open country, for the prairie, hills, and mountains he called home.

Suddenly, above the hubbub, Fargo heard his name called loud and clear. He glanced into the street and saw Marshal Fedder mounted on a bay.

"Come with me. There's been another one."

Pushing through to a hitching rail, Fargo saw the deep pain in the lawman's eyes. "No," he said softly.

"I just got word," the lawman said. Leaning down, he offered his arm. "Climb on. We'll ride double."

The streets they took were streets Fargo knew all to well. They brought him to the boardinghouse, where yet another crowd had formed and was being held at bay by a pair of husky deputies. Marshal Fedder rode right up the walk to the porch and drew rein as the doctor shuffled out the screen door.

For Fargo, it was a nightmare made real. "How bad is it?" he asked, sliding down.

"You have to see for yourself," the sawbones answered. "Words can't describe it."

The young deputy, Bonham, was in the main hall, his forehead pressed to the wall, his skin as white as a sheet. "It's horrible," he was saying over and over.

Fargo dogged the marshal's steps. He saw a puddle of blood spreading out from the kitchen, before he saw the body. Girding himself, he stepped to the doorway.

Erica Dunn had been in the act of making her evening meal when her attacker came up behind her, apparently after sneaking in through the back door. She had been savagely beaten to the floor and there subjected to torture few had ever known. Her nose and ears had been cut off, her body mutilated beyond recognition. Fargo saw her severed tongue lying partially under the stove. He tasted bile and turned away. Whoever had done that must be made to pay.

"There's one more," Bonham told them. "Down that side hall."

A wide red smear led from the junction to Dunn's bedroom. On his slit belly on the floor lay the store clerk, Metz, one arm flung toward a closed window, the other hand clamped in vain over an eight-inch cut at the base of his throat.

"He must have heard something and come downstairs to investigate," Marshal Fedder speculated. "The killer gutted him, then opened his neck and stood around gloating while he crawled in here to try to escape."

"Two more," Fargo said, half to himself.

"It was the breed," Fedder said. "I'd stake my life on it."

Fargo walked outside and took a seat on the porch. The brisk evening breeze failed to cool the fire burning out of control in his breast. He had never wanted to kill another human being so much as he did at that very moment. The screen door banged and the lawman was at his side.

"I'll go question Morgan, but we both know what he'll say. He probably fired Charley Crow this morning, so he's not responsible for anything the breed does."

"He's responsible, all right," Fargo growled. "And by God, he's going to pay."

"When do you leave with those teachers you were telling me about?"

"Tomorrow."

Marshal Fedder bent, reached into his boot, and pulled out a knuckle-duster, a small, heavy .32-caliber derringer that lacked a barrel and could be used as a bludgeon when the need arose. "Here. It's the least I can do. I can always get another."

Fargo was about to decline, to say that he had no use for a gun that was only accurate up to a range of five yards, that he had seldom relied on derringers and saw no need to start, but one look at the haunted lawman changed his mind. "Thanks," he said. "It might just come in handy."

Little did he know.

7

The constant sniffling and whining about drove Fargo crazy. For close to two full days he had listened to Ernest Squib moan and groan about the atrocious climate in that part of the country. For almost two days he had been forced to put up with the man blowing his nose every sixty seconds with a sound that resembled the bugle cry of a male elk in rut. And as if that weren't enough torture for anyone to have to endure, he'd had to abide Squib's constant complaining.

But enough was enough. Fargo reined up on the crest of a low ridge and shifted in the saddle to regard the schoolteacher coldly.

Squib had yet another of his apparently endless supply of handkerchiefs pressed to his red nose and was doing his best to drive every female elk within five miles into a romantic dither. He wiped his nose, made another disgusted sound when he cleared his throat, and piped up with, "God, this is unbearable! I don't know if it's all this grass or our smelly animals or what, but I feel as if I could just die."

"Do it," Fargo said.

Squib sniffed. "I beg your pardon?"

"Do us a big favor. Go ahead and die," Fargo clarified. "At least we won't have to put up with your bellyaching."

Elizabeth Langtree laughed, but Felicia Taugner got her hackles up and declared, "That's a perfectly terrible thing to say to someone, Mr. Fargo. Poor Ernest is doing the best he can, given the circumstances. Can he help it if he has such a delicate constitution?"

"That's right," Squib said in his own defense. "I was born this way. My mother says I was a frail baby and I just never got any better. You should pity me."

"The only one I pity is me, having to put up with your nonsense," Fargo said. "It's distracting me when I should be paying attention to our surroundings. Every time he blows his nose, our lives are at risk."

Felicia tittered. "How utterly ridiculous! For a frontiersman, you have an extraordinary imagination."

"Ridiculous, is it?" Fargo refused to back down. "Lady, sounds carry far out here, much farther than they do back where you come from. Hostile Indians, outlaws, grizzlies, you name it, might hear his racket and decide to come see what it's all about. And if I'm being distracted, I might not notice them until it's too late."

"We're no more than forty miles from Denver," Felicia said. "Surely we're not in any danger yet."

"We were in danger the minute we left the town limits," Fargo corrected her.

Ernest Squib was searching his pockets for another handkerchief. "I'm sorry to be such a bother, Mr. Fargo," he said, "but I honestly don't see what else I can do. I am, however, open to suggestions."

"Fine," Fargo said. "I know a trick that might work." Dismounting, he stepped into the high grass and broke off a handful of stems, which he then broke into pieces about six inches long. Going over to Squib, he handed them up. "Stuff these in your shirt pockets."

The schoolteacher looked at them as if the stems carried the Black Plague. "You can't be serious. You know how grass sets me off."

"Do it," Fargo commanded.

Reluctantly, Squib obeyed. The stems were so long, the tops poked out from his pockets. "Anything else?" he asked sarcastically.

"Yes," Fargo said, and nodded at the sorrel's damp neck. "Wipe your hand on your horse."

"What are you about?" Squib asked as he did what Fargo suggested. He scrunched up his nose and mouth when he saw the thick layer of sweat caking his palm.

"Now rub that on your cheeks and chin," Fargo directed.

Squib gasped. "Are you insane? Are you deliberately trying to kill me?"

Felicia Taugner urged her mount nearer. "Don't listen to him, Ernest. He's just having fun at your expense."

"No, I'm trying to cure him," Fargo said. He tapped Squib's elbow. "Now do it."

Timidly, the man complied, his lips trembling, but whether from fear or loathing it was hard to say. When he was done, he blanched, then hacked violently for a few moments.

"See?" Felicia scolded Skye. "You're making him suffer needlessly. Stop this silly nonsense this moment."

Squib nodded and inhaled deeply. "I have to agree with her. You're punishing me for a condition over which I have no control. It's not fair, sir, and I most vigorously protest." He went to wipe his sleeve on his chin.

Fargo grabbed the teacher's wrist and held firm. "Listen to me," he said. "When a man is thrown by a horse, the best thing for him to do is get right back on. Or if someone is scared of the dark, the only cure is for them to go out at night and walk around until they see there's nothing to be afraid of—"

"You're mixing apples and oranges," Felicia interrupted. "He has a physical ailment, not an emotional difficulty."

Fargo ignored her. "If a man breaks a leg, he doesn't lie in bed the rest of his life. He has to get up and around, exercise the leg so it will heal faster. Or if someone is stabbed or shot, it's better to have fresh air than be cooped up in a room forever."

"I think I see what you're trying to say," Squib said. "But I don't think you truly appreciate the gravity of what you are asking me to do."

"I'm asking you to ride behind the packhorses for the rest of the day," Fargo said, moving to the Ovaro.

"At the rear?" Felicia said. "That's where the dust is the very worst."

"I know," Fargo said.

"Oh, my!" Squib exclaimed. He sniffled a few times, then squared his shoulders and wheeled the sorrel. Saying half under his breath. "I'm doomed, doomed, doomed," he rode toward the back of the line.

"Don't do it!" Felicia urged.

Fargo stepped into the stirrups. "Let him go," he advised. "You won't do him any favors by mothering him." Clucking the stallion into motion, he resumed their trek. It surprised him that Squib had the gumption to do as he requested. It also surprised him that Elizabeth Langtree hadn't sided with Felicia Taugner, although it shouldn't.

The differences between the two schoolmarms ran deeper than the way they looked. Felicia was a practical woman who kept her emotions under tight control. She rarely laughed, hardly ever smiled. Elizabeth, on the other hand, loved to have fun, to relax and enjoy life. When they stopped at night, she was the one who kept Fargo grinning with stories about her childhood in Ohio and some of the men she had known.

Fargo found himself liking Langtree a lot. But as yet he had not let on. He had something else on his mind—namely, watching their back trail for a sign of Morgan's pack of ruthless killers. He was sure they would show sooner or later. So far, though, there had been no trace of the butchers.

Another fact weighed heavily on Fargo's mind. The sole reason he had agreed to serve as a guide was to get to the bottom of the mystery that had resulted in the deaths of three innocent people. In some way, those grisly murders were linked to the schoolteachers. How, he couldn't say yet, but before their journey was over he would know the answer.

From the ridge they descended onto a broad plain. To their left, to the west, reared rolling foothills, and beyond the hills towered the craggy ramparts known as the Rocky Mountains, foremost among them majestic Long's Peak, named after an early explorer.

Shortly before sundown Fargo halted in a strip of willows and cottonwoods lining a crystal-clear river fed by runoff from the high country. In a glade bounded by wildflowers he decided to set up camp.

Elizabeth Langtree stepped to the water's edge and raised her arms to the heavens. "Smell those flowers! Listen to the river! Look at those peaks! I had no idea this land could be so incredibly beautiful."

"You haven't seen anything yet," Fargo said, leading the Ovaro to drink. "After you're all settled into your new job, have someone take you up into the Bighorn Mountains. You'll never want to go back East again."

The raven-haired beauty grinned. "I've noticed that the men

out here are a lot like the mountains—tall, rugged, and good looking. I wonder how a girl goes about getting someone like you interested in her?"

Once again she was making her interest plain, and Fargo, weakening, was about to say something he might later regret, when up rode Ernest Squib. The man swayed in the saddle as if drunk and uttered a gurgling whine. His face was beet red and as puffy as an overripe melon. His nose was running, and he was caked with dust.

"Goodness!" Felicia said, staring hard at Fargo. "Look at the poor man. Look at what you've done to him."

"How do you feel, Ernest?" Elizabeth asked.

"Dead," Squib replied, and slid stiffly to the grass. "I've swallowed more dust in the past few hours than I have food since the day I was born." Moaning pitiably, he sank to his knees and feebly splashed water onto his face and forearms. "I don't think your cure will work, Mr. Fargo."

"Try it again tomorrow," Fargo suggested. "Another day might be all it takes."

"To put me in an early grave? I agree." Squib bent low and dunked his whole head into the river.

Since none of the teachers knew the first thing about stripping off saddles and packs, Fargo busied himself piling their supplies close to the fire Elizabeth made, and then tethered the horses.

Felicia observed him closely. "Why do you bother tying them at night? It seems to me they won't wander very far from all this water and grass."

"It's not the stock we have to worry about," Fargo said. "Next to counting coup, Indians most love to steal horses from whites. Even friendly Indians will try it if they think they can get away with it." He gestured at the vegetation. "And if a grizzly or a mountain lion roams on by and our horses catch the scent, they're likely to stampede and not stop until they've gone all the way to Denver." He paused. "The old-time trappers had a saying that still applies. It's better to count a horse's ribs than its tracks."

"What about supper?" she asked.

The night before they had eaten canned goods, but their supply was limited. Since Fargo preferred fresh meat, he took the

Sharps and hiked westward along the riverbank, seeking game. He saw several ducks but left them alone. A raccoon waddled off at his approach. And finally he came on a large rabbit chewing on sweet grass near the water's edge. A single shot did the trick.

"You've killed a bunny!" Felicia Taugner declared on seeing Fargo return with the dead rabbit dangling from one hand. "I used to raise them when I was a girl. How could you?"

"I like to eat now and then," Fargo said, placing the limp animal on top of a large, flat rock. Drawing the Arkansas toothpick, he proceeded to skin it and chopped the meat into fit pieces for the pot.

Half an hour later the tangy scent of boiling stew filled the clearing. Felicia walked over, her expression contrite. "Sorry I picked on you. That does smell delicious, and I'm famished."

"Pass out the bowls and spoons and we'll dig in," Fargo said. He ladled portions for each of them, then sat back against his saddle with his own bowl in his lap. By now twilight had claimed the landscape, and off in the distance a coyote wailed.

"How lonesome it sounds," Felicia said.

"I know the feeling," Elizabeth commented, but she didn't elaborate.

Ernest Squib tore into his supper with relish, hardly bothering to chew. He ate two big helpings. As he bent forward to set his bowl down, he gave out with a tremendous belch. Squib blushed and blurted, "My humble apologies. I don't know what came over me. All this frontier living is turning me into a primitive."

"That will be the day," Fargo joked. He happened to glance to the south and swore he saw movement at the very limits of his vision. It was too dark for him to be certain, but he thought he glimpsed a horse and rider.

"Will it be the same at the settlements?" Squib asked, pushing his bowler hat back on his nearly bald head.

"About the same," Fargo answered. "High winds are a problem all year long. And once it snows in the fall, you're liable to have snow on the ground until spring."

"You make it sound like the North Pole," Felicia scoffed.

"When the first blizzard of the season buries you under ten feet of white stuff, you'll think that it is," Fargo mentioned while surveying the plain in the direction of Denver. The rider had disappeared but Fargo wasn't fooled. Someone was tracking them. His money was on the breed or the mountain man.

"Ten feet?" Squib repeated. "I haven't seen that much snow at one time since I was a kid. I'd sit and watch it fall for hours." He coughed. "My mother would never let me go out and play in it like all the other kids were allowed to do. She claimed it was bad for my health."

Fargo sipped his coffee while the teachers chatted about their childhoods. Felicia, it turned out, had been raised in a poor section of New York City and struggled to make something of herself. Elizabeth had been the pampered pet of a well-to-do family. She had scandalized her parents by choosing a teaching career.

It wasn't long before the three were ready to turn in. Unaccustomed as they were to spending long hours in the saddle, they were extremely tired at the end of each day. Fargo knew they would toughen in time, but he was glad they weren't going to sit up late swapping stories. He had something to do.

Ernest fell asleep first, the second his head hit the pillow. Felicia dozed off next, lying prim and straight on her back, her hands neatly folded on top of her blanket. Elizabeth was the last. For the longest while she gazed at Fargo across the fire. Whenever he glanced at her, she would close her eyes and pretend to be asleep. But he wasn't fooled. He could tell by her breathing when she eventually fell asleep for real.

Fargo waited another fifteen minutes to be sure none of them was going to wake up any time soon. Placing his tin cup down, he grabbed the Sharps and rose. He remembered to remove his spurs before he crept into the night.

Once beyond the glow from the fire, Fargo moved faster, traveling in a wide loop that would bring him close to the spot where he had seen the rider. He had not gone more than fifty yards when the heavy stomp of a hoof from somewhere ahead alerted him to the fact the rider had swung around to the west.

Like a ghost, Fargo flitted from tree to tree. It was sloppy of Charley Crow or Graven to come so close. They were too confident for their own good, and he was going to see that they paid for their mistake.

Then a pair of silhouettes appeared, driving Fargo to the

ground. They were horses, not men. He realized there had been two riders, probably the breed *and* the mountain man. Listening with his head cocked for the slightest sound, Fargo waited for them to betray their presence.

Minutes dragged by as if weighted with anchors. Fargo became impatient, a fatal flaw if not held in check. He snaked closer, careful to make no noise. One of the horses stomped the ground again, as horses often did when they wanted to graze but were tied too far from grass, or when their owners had tied them and gone off and they wanted to be loose.

The thought sent a chill of apprehension down Fargo's spine. It suddenly dawned on him that Charley Crow and Graven might not be there, that while he had been stalking toward them, they had been *stalking toward the teachers*.

Galvanized into action, Fargo rose and spun. He ran when he should have walked, fearing he was too late, that the breed had already slit the throat of all three or Graven had throttled them in their sleep. His concern made him reckless. He skirted a clump of high weeds, darted past a thorny bush, and reached a stretch of grass that rose as high as his waist.

The next moment a human form popped up directly in front of him. Fargo was so close that he had no time to stop or swing aside. He saw the man begin to turn toward him. Then they collided and Fargo lost his grip on the Sharps. No sooner did his shoulder hit the earth than he palmed the Arkansas toothpick and sprang. A silent kill was called for, in order not to alert the other cutthroat.

The man crumpled like soggy toast, offering no resistance other than a frightened squawk. The cry saved his life, because Fargo discerned in an instant that the wriggling bundle of panic under him wasn't Charley Crow or Graven. He shoved the man flat and held the tip of the toothpick to his throat.

"Don't move!" Fargo snarled.

"No, sir," came the frightened reply. "Just don't hurt me, please. I don't mean you any harm."

The voice was familiar. Fargo straddled the man's chest and looked down in disbelief on the pale features of Edwards, the desk clerk from the Imperial Hotel. "What the hell are you doing here?" he demanded.

Evidently the clerk recognized him at the same second.

"You! What's the idea, mister?" Edwards blustered. "You have no right to attack me like a damned savage. I wasn't doing anything."

Fargo slid off but held the knife ready for use. "You've been following my party since we left Denver, haven't you?"

"Maybe I have, maybe I haven't," Edwards said. "It's a free country. I can go anywhere I damn please, and there's not a thing you can do about it."

"Save that talk for back in town," Fargo said. "You're in the middle of nowhere now. I could kill you and no one would ever know."

"You wouldn't dare," Edwards said, without conviction. He slowly sat up, revealing a holster strapped to his waist. It looked as out of place on him as ballet tights would on a lumberjack.

Fargo plucked the clerk's revolver out. "A Smith and Wesson," he noted. "Ever shot a gun before?"

"Once," Edwards declared. "At a tin can six feet away. I hit it, too!"

"Was it charging you at the time with a tomahawk in its hand?"

"What?"

"Never mind." Fargo replaced the toothpick, then studied the bumbling incompetent. "You're right. I can't force you to tell me why you're here. But it would be in your own best interest."

"How do you figure, mister? I don't know you from Adam. For all I know, you're as trustworthy as a patent medicine drummer." Edwards shook his head. "No, thanks. I'll just go on about my business and leave you to yours."

"Do you intend to follow us farther?" Fargo asked. Edwards didn't respond, but the fact that the man clammed up was all the answer Fargo needed. "This country isn't safe. For your own sake, why don't you ride with us? I'm sure the teachers won't mind."

"No, thanks. I'd rather be by myself."

"Whatever you want," Fargo said, rising. "But you're making a big mistake. I know how to live off the land. You don't. I can keep you alive."

Edwards hesitated. He glanced off through the trees at the

flickering campfire and opened his mouth as if to say something. Instead, he shook his head.

Fargo tried one more time. It wasn't that he felt obligated to protect the clerk, since the man had treated him with nothing but scorn since they met. He wanted Edwards close, where he could keep an eye on him, rather than slinking along behind them. "Wouldn't you rather spend time with a couple of pretty ladies than be all by yourself?" Fargo remembered something. "I thought you were fond of Felicia. Here's your chance to get to know her really well."

"I already do," Edwards said, and recoiled as if he had blundered.

Fargo thought he had the man figured out. "I saw the two of you leave the hotel one time. How long were you seeing one another?"

"That was our first and only date," Edwards said, and even in the dark his face lit up. "We went out to eat. It was the happiest moment of my life when she asked me to go."

"Is she the reason you're here?" Fargo probed, thinking it would be just like the love-struck fool to pull such a hare-brained stunt.

"None of your business."

"I won't hold it against you," Fargo fibbed. "But she might, when I tell her."

The clerk grabbed Fargo's arm. "Please, no! If she found out, she'd be furious with me. Don't say a word to her. I give you my word that you won't see hide nor hair of me until we reach Banner."

"Why there?" Fargo wondered.

Before Edwards could answer, the night was rent by a shriek of terror coming from the glade where Fargo had made camp, a shriek that was drowned out by the thunderous roar of a roving beast mingled with the high-pitched squeals of frantic horses.

8

Skye Fargo was in motion while the woman's shriek still wavered on the night air. Whirling, he sped toward camp, plowing through patches of dense brush instead of going around. Limbs tugged at his legs, branches tore at his buckskins.

The bawling roar told Fargo that the nocturnal prowler was a bear. He worried that it might be a grizzly, that one of the massive monsters had wandered down from the high country and been drawn to the glade by the scent of their horses, or the scent of the teachers themselves.

Fargo had no illusions about the ability of the schoolmarms and the schoolmaster to protect themselves. The bear would rip through them like a butcher knife through sticks of butter. They didn't stand a chance.

As Fargo drew nearer, the racket increased. The horses were whinnying in a terror-stricken frenzy. He saw figures moving about and heard one of the women empty her lungs in a drawn-out scream. Tucking the stock of the Sharps to his shoulder, he burst into the open and halted to take in the chaotic scene.

Felicia Taugner stood riveted with fear over by the fire, her blanket pulled as high as her chin, as if she were trying to hide behind it.

Elizabeth Langtree brandished a burning branch, which she had pulled from the fire but was wisely making no attempt to use.

Ernest Squib still sat on the ground, frozen in shock, his mouth wide open as if to catch moths.

The five pack animals and the mounts were frantically trying to rip free of their tether ropes. The Ovaro had almost succeeded and was rearing again and again.

And over by the pile of supplies stood the intruder, an enormous black bear more interested in rummaging for something to eat than in attacking anyone or anything. Fargo let himself relax a little, since black bears were rarely dangerous unless they were provoked or were protecting cubs. He pointed the rifle at the ground, figuring a shot would scare it off.

To Fargo's amazement, Elizabeth Langtree suddenly dashed up behind the animal and rammed the burning branch into its flank. The bear let out a squalling bellow and spun, accidentally knocking her over as it did. Then, without warning, it barreled across the glade toward the sanctuary of the woodland. But in so doing, it rushed straight at Skye Fargo.

"Look out!" Felicia cried.

Fargo wasn't about to be caught flat-footed. He leaped aside with space to spare, and the black bear hurtled on past him. Felicia cried out again, which he thought was silly of her since he was safe. The next moment he discovered that she had been yelling at someone else.

A pistol blasted behind him. Fargo turned in time to see Edwards with the smoking Smith and Wesson in hand. The clerk had followed him. And now, rather than jump out of the bear's way as Fargo had done, Edwards had tried to shoot it in the head. Bear skulls, though, were notoriously thick. A single shot seldom sufficed. In this instance the black bear never slowed. It slammed into Edwards with the force of a runaway steam engine, batting him aside with a single swipe of its huge paw.

Edwards howled as he went down. The black bear kept on going into the undergrowth, yowling madly from its wounds.

Fargo let the bear go. It hadn't bothered the horses or the teachers, and had only felled the clerk in self-defense. He ran to Edwards and sank to one knee. "How bad—," he began, and stopped because he could see the answer for himself.

The bear's long claws had opened the hapless clerk from the sternum to the crotch, shearing through his clothes and his flesh as easily as might a sword through wax. Blood streamed from four of the slash marks, soaking the man's shirt.

Edwards was in shock. He had risen on his elbows and gaped at the wounds, making no effort to staunch the flow of blood. "Oh, God!" he whined. "I'm a dead man."

Fargo knew they must act swiftly or the clerk would die. "Boil water!" he shouted at Felicia, then he stooped and lifted the clerk to carry him closer to the fire. Edwards made no objection. "Hang on," Fargo coaxed. "Maybe it's not as bad as it seems."

The only response was a forlorn whimper.

Squib collected his wits and shoved upright. He spread out one of his own blankets, saying, "Put him here."

"Oh, I hurt," Edwards said as Fargo laid him down. The clerk tried to double over and cover the slashes with his arms, but Fargo stopped him.

"We need to examine them." Fargo unbuttoned the top three buttons of the shirt and lifted the drenched cotton high enough to peer underneath. Two of the gashes were over an inch wide, and Fargo saw intestines bulging from the abdominal cavity.

Elizabeth hastened over, brushing herself off. She was unhurt, except for a bruise on her arm. "Who is he? Is he all right? I was only trying to scare the bear off. I didn't mean for anyone to be harmed."

"We need to stitch him up, fast," Fargo said. "Do you or Felicia have a large sewing needle?"

"I don't," Elizabeth said, and glanced at Taugner.

"Sorry," Felicia said, in the act of setting a pot of water on the fire. "A few small ones is all I have."

"Then we do it the hard way," Fargo said. Indians often fashioned needles from bones, and he could do the same. It would be simple to make a crude one from the leg bones of the rabbit he had slain. For thread he would have to use whangs clipped off his buckskin shirt. It was the best he could do under the circumstances. He went to rise.

"No," Edwards said, clutching at Fargo's leg. "Don't bother. It's too late."

"It's never too late," Fargo said, placing a hand on the man's shoulder.

"Where there is life, there's hope," Squib anxiously threw in. "Rest assured we will do all in our power to save you."

"It's too late," Edwards said. A sharp cry escaped his lips, and he abruptly arched his back, gritting his teeth against the agony racking him.

Fargo tore at the shirt, aware they must stem the blood loss

86

swiftly. Edwards grabbed one of his wrists and clung on with astounding strength, preventing him from finishing. "You've got to let us help," Fargo urged.

"Too late," Edwards reiterated, and shook from head to toe. "I don't have much time left."

The blanket under the clerk was covered with blood. Squib's lips moved silently, perhaps in prayer.

"Why?" Edwards asked of no one in particular. "Why now? Why here?" His dilated eyes focused on Fargo. "The story of my life. I finally find happiness, and I die. I'd laugh if it didn't hurt so much."

"Be still," Fargo said. "Let me try and sew up those cuts."

Edwards weakly shook his head, his hand falling to his side. "Don't bother," he mumbled.

Fargo refused to listen. The man had lost an awful amount of blood, and the claws might have punctured an internal organ, but Fargo was not going to give up. He'd seen men survive much graver wounds. Fingers flying, he unbuttoned the shirt enough to expose the damage.

"Damn!" Squib declared, looking as if he would be sick.

Fargo twisted to go check on the water, but Edwards grasped at his arm.

"Please. Do something for me. Contact my sister, Edna Edwards, in Evanston, Illinois. She's all the family I have left. I don't want her wondering what ever became of me." His grip tightened. "Promise me, mister. I want your word that you'll let her know."

It was too late to do anything to save him, Fargo realized. The body had about bled dry, and when the clerk breathed there was a sucking sound, as from a perforated lung. "I give you my word," he said softly.

"Thanks. You're not so bad, after all." Edwards swiveled his head until he faced the schoolmarms. Smiling, he said, "For a little while you gave my life meaning. For that, I'm forever grateful. I just wish we'd had more time."

"Do you mean me?" Felicia said. "All we did was go out to eat."

"That's not all," Edwards said, sounding upset. "I came this far, didn't I? I would have gone all the way to the—to the—" His voice broke and he went into violent convulsions.

Fargo tried to hold him down, to keep him from rolling into the fire, but needed Squib's help. Edwards gnashed his teeth, groaning loudly, his mouth flecked with spittle. His body snapped rigid, and for a few seconds he stared at the schoolmarms.

"I did like you wanted. It's—"

Again the clerk choked off, only this time his body sagged, lifeless, onto the sodden blanket.

"He passed out. Tell me he just passed out," Elizabeth said, aghast, a hand to her throat.

Fargo shook his head and rose. Taking a spare blanket from their supplies, he covered the dead man, then stepped back. "He was in the wrong place at the wrong time."

"Who was he?" Ernest Squib asked.

Felicia responded. "I can answer that. His name was Larry Edwards. He was a desk clerk at the Hotel Imperial, where the two of you stayed the night before we left Denver. He and I went to supper once." She sadly shook her head. "A nice enough man, but not my type. What do you suppose he was doing way out here?"

"The man wouldn't say," Fargo said, his suspicions rekindled. In his opinion, Edwards would not have left Denver without a good reason, which had to be linked to Taugner. She was the one who had dated him, and Edwards had been looking in her direction when he made his last puzzling remarks. What had the man meant by his statement that he had done as she wanted? Fargo wondered.

"What do we do now? Take him back to town?" Squib asked.

"We bury him and go on," Fargo said.

"Just like that?"

"Just like that." Fargo returned to their provisions. It hadn't occurred to him to bring a shovel, but there had to be something he could use to dig a grave.

Squib did not appear satisfied. "I don't know. It seems to me that we should do the right thing and transport the body to Denver for a decent burial. I'd want the same done for me."

"I agree," Elizabeth said.

"Well, I don't," Felicia spoke up. "For one thing, we're expected in the settlements. For another, funerals cost money and none of us are millionaires. Which one of you is willing to foot the bill?"

Neither of the others replied.

"That settles it," Felicia said. "We do as Mr. Fargo wants and give him the best burial we can right here."

Fargo found several picket pins he had brought along to use when they camped on the open plain. He handed one to each of the teachers, then stepped to a spot well back from the river and began digging with his own. "Don't stand there like bumps on a log," he chided the teachers. "Get to work."

For over half an hour the four of them chipped away at the hard earth, scooping out a shallow grave. Fargo and Squib toted the body to the hole.

"Shouldn't we check his pockets?" Ernest suggested. "There might be something of value for his sister to have."

Squatting, Fargo rummaged under the blanket, his hand growing slick with sticky blood. In a shirt pocket was a pencil. In a pants pocket were a key and several coins. Fargo reached into the second pocket and felt his fingers close on a folded wad of money. He pulled it out, thinking that the clerk must have robbed a bank, until he learned most of the bills were small denominations. Edwards had left the world with under fifty dollars to his name.

"What about his horse?" Elizabeth said. "Surely he didn't walk all this way?"

"First we cover him," Fargo said. Over a layer of dirt they spread as many small rocks as they could find to deter scavengers. Not satisfied, Fargo had them gather dead branches and added the limbs to the mound. Then, the Sharps in hand, he headed west. "I'll be back in a bit."

"What if the bear comes back?" Felicia called out.

"It won't."

"But what if it does?"

"Scream real loud."

Retracing his steps to where the clerk had left the two horses, Fargo unraveled the reins of a saddled chestnut gelding and walked the animals toward the camp. He could have ridden but he needed time to ponder.

It seemed that the more involved Fargo became with the whole affair, the more of a mystery it became. Why was Frederick Morgan interested in the teachers? Why had Morgan tried to have him killed? Why had Larry Edwards trailed them north? There were so many questions and too few answers.

Squib and the women were ringed around the fire when Fargo arrived. They jumped up on hearing him and leveled the rifles he had bought before leaving Denver so they would be able to defend themselves. "It's only me," he assured them to prevent a nervous finger from twitching.

Fargo added the clerk's animals to the string. He removed everything from the packhorse—mainly food supplies and odds and ends like matches and a compass. Also included were three canteens, new models from back East. Only one sloshed when Fargo gave it a light shake.

The schoolmarms and the schoolmaster were huddled close to the fire. Fargo joined them and poured himself a cup of strong black coffee. The three looked at him as if they had something to say, so he piped up with, "Well?"

"We were wondering," Squib said. "You took that poor man's death in stride, as if you have seen a lot of people die. Is that how it is out here? Is it as bad as the newspapers would have us believe?"

"Having second thoughts?" Fargo asked, not trying to be sarcastic. He couldn't blame them if they were. The teachers were as out of place in the West as fish out of water. In the settlements they would do all right, provided they were spared the horrors of Indian raids and did not run afoul of roving outlaws. "I'll take you back to Denver if you are."

"Not on your life," Elizabeth Langtree declared. "Yes, I was deeply moved by that man's passing, but I'm not about to let it spoil the adventure of a lifetime."

Felicia was gazing into her coffee cup. "You didn't answer Ernest, Mr. Fargo," she commented.

"Life out here can be tough at times," Fargo admitted. "But no one ever claimed that living on the frontier would be easy. Maybe in fifty years, when this whole territory has been settled, things will quiet down. Until then, every time you leave civilization behind, you take your life into your hands."

"Wonderful," Squib muttered.

Elizabeth glanced at their stacked supplies. "What will we

do about all the stuff that belonged to Larry Edwards? We can't just keep it. That would be unethical."

"We can sell everything for a fair price and wire the money to his sister," Fargo proposed. "There're bound to be people in Banner, Wyarno, or Bighorn who will take everything off our hands."

"What a nice idea," Elizabeth said in a tone that implied he was ripe for sainthood.

Fargo shrugged and went on sipping his coffee. The teachers finished theirs in silence and turned in. Fargo would have liked to do the same, since they had another long day ahead of them, but he hardly felt tired. Two more cups of coffee didn't help matters much.

Eventually Fargo stood and walked the perimeter of the clearing. A sweep of the horizon in all directions failed to turn up any other campfires. The horses had quieted down long ago, and most were dozing. He stopped to rub the Ovaro's neck, then ambled to the river and watched the murky water swirl past. In the distance a wolf howled.

"It's so peaceful at this time of night, isn't it?"

Fargo turned, upset with himself for not having heard Elizabeth approach—even if her footsteps had been masked by the sound of the swiftly flowing water and the wolf. "What are you doing out of bed?" he asked testily. "You need all the sleep you can get."

The raven-haired beauty sauntered closer and regarded him quizzically. "Most men would be glad to see me."

"I'm not most men," Fargo said, facing away from her. The last thing he needed was for her to throw herself at him again. It was getting harder to ignore her hints, to say nothing of her voluptuous body.

"So I've noticed," Elizabeth said. "You're a rarity—a man who knows his own mind and acts as he damn well pleases, no matter what others think."

Fargo looked at her. "Have me all figured out, do you?"

"Not entirely, but I'm working on it." Elizabeth smiled and folded her arms across her chest. In the process, she accented her breasts, which pushed against her dress as if trying to burst free.

Since she had no intentions of listening to him, Fargo decided to pry. "What can you tell me about your friend Felicia?"

"I don't know her all that well," Elizabeth said. "We were put in touch with one another after we answered the ad for teachers. I didn't meet her in person until I stepped off the stage in Denver."

"The same with Squib?"

"Yes. Why all the questions?"

"No reason," Fargo hedged. The wind shifted, filling his nostrils with the heady scent of her perfume. A familiar twitching in his loins made him turn toward the river and crouch to splash water on his face. The next thing he knew, warm fingers stroked the nape of his neck.

"Why don't you like me, Skye? Most men do."

Standing, Fargo pivoted and found himself nose to nose with her. She wore a teasing grin, her mouth puckered seductively. "Are you sure that you're a schoolmarm?"

Elizabeth blinked, then laughed. She promptly covered her mouth to keep from waking the others. "My, my. A refined sense of humor to go with your rugged good looks. What more could any woman ask for?"

"You really should turn in," Fargo said, feeling ridiculous turning her away when what he really wanted to do was take her in his arms and mash her sensuous form against his. "I'll be going to bed shortly."

"But I don't want to." Elizabeth held her ground. Her grin widening, she brazenly moved forward so that her folded arms pressed against his chest. "And I can't believe that you truly want me to go."

Fargo swore he could feel the tips of her breasts through his shirt, which was impossible. He suddenly became warm all over, his skin prickling as if from a rash. When he went to speak, his throat was so constricted he had to cough to clear it.

"Catching a cold, handsome?" Elizabeth baited him. She leaned nearer, her warm breath fanning his cheeks.

Just when Fargo was set to lean over and plant his mouth on hers, a loud splash came from upriver and one of the horses nickered. Immediately several stood and stared westward. Thankful for the interruption, Fargo hefted the Sharps and moved toward the string, saying, "Something is out there. You'd better stay close to the fire."

Her disappointment apparent, the schoolmarm obeyed.

Fargo calmed the horses while listening for the splash to be repeated. It could have been a fish or a frog, he reflected, but the reaction of the horses pointed at something else. The wind picked up, rustling the cottonwoods and making it hard for him to hear other sounds.

As usual, Fargo relied on his pinto. So long as the stallion stood and stared off into the darkness, he was convinced there was something out there. Twice he thought he detected the crackle of underbrush. He was strongly tempted to go into the woods after it but was reluctant to leave the teachers alone again.

Hunkering down, Fargo waited, hoping the creature, or person, would come to him. Hidden among the horses, he would be hard to spot.

The minutes went by slowly. Somewhere an owl hooted, and from far off wavered the unnerving scream of a mountain lion.

Finally the Ovaro lowered its head and nipped at the grass. Fargo walked to the fire and sat down. Elizabeth was under the covers, sound asleep. He poured the last of the coffee into his cup and leaned back.

So far the trip had not gone well, and Fargo's intuition told him the worst was yet to come. Somewhere between there and the Bighorns, Frederick Morgan would show his hand. Fargo had to be ready.

Felicia Taugner turned over in her sleep and mumbled a few words. Then, as clear as could be, she said, "Larry! Where did you put them?" She mumbled a while longer, sighed, and fell silent.

Fargo drained his cup. Did her words have any meaning, he asked himself, or was she just dreaming? He stayed awake as long as he could, wishing she would say more. The fire had dwindled to tiny fingers of flame when he spread out on his back and pulled his hat brim down over his eyes. He needed rest. Dawn would come soon enough, and he had to stay alert all day long. Any lapse on his part and he'd wind up just like Larry Edwards—worm food.

9

The very next day Elizabeth Langtree started in on Fargo again. They had no sooner broke camp and forded the river than she goaded her horse up alongside the Ovaro and smiled seductively at him. "We never did finish our little chat last night. What was out there, anyway?"

"Probably an animal," Fargo said.

"Probably?" Elizabeth repeated. "Are you expecting someone else to show up out of the blue like Edwards did?"

Fargo had been debating how much to tell her, and Squib. Their lives would be at risk, too, if Morgan's bunch put in an appearance. But he didn't know which one of them, if either, he could trust. As for Felicia, since she had been the only one of the three in Denver when the killing started, and since Dixie Lee had all but mentioned her by name when questioning him, he suspected that she might have something to do with the cause of all the trouble. He trusted her about as far as he could heave the Ovaro.

"Let's hope not," Fargo said, deciding to play it safe and not give any of them the benefit of the doubt until they proved themselves trustworthy. He'd live longer that way.

Elizabeth tossed her head so that her glorious mane swished around her shoulders. "Well, I just hope we're not interrupted the next time we have some time to ourselves."

"Some women can't take a hint," Fargo muttered, and listened to her gay mirth as she trotted back to ride beside Felicia. At the rear of the line rode Ernest Squib, a bandanna Fargo had lent him covering his mouth and nose. He waved when Fargo looked his way.

By the middle of the afternoon they were among low hills. Fargo hoped to reach the Cache la Poudre river before night-

94

fall, but they fell short by a good eight miles. In a basin watered by a small stream they set up camp for the night. Supper provided itself in the form of a young doe Fargo dropped at two hundred yards.

After the meal, Fargo left the teachers and hiked to the rise south of the stream. From there he enjoyed a sweeping panoramic view. In the middle of the day a person would be able to see clear to Denver, but at twilight objects more than a few miles off were obscured by haze and encroaching darkness.

Fargo scanned the landscape thoroughly and was satisfied no one was on their trail. Then he went to turn, and a last shaft of sunlight reflected off of a metallic object not two miles distant. It was as if a tiny star flared to life in the middle of the vast prairie. But Fargo knew better. The flash had been made by a spur or a bridle or a gun. Someone was definitely back there.

Three guesses who, Fargo mused. He had two choices that he could see. Either he did nothing and continued on until they were overtaken, or he snuck on back there to prove his hunch right and do whatever needed doing.

The schoolmarms were giggling like two little girls when Fargo walked into camp and over to the horse string. He threw on his saddle blanket and was lifting his saddle when Squib noticed.

"Say, what are you doing? Are you going somewhere?"

"For a short ride," Fargo said. With a deft flip, he positioned the saddle on the broad back of the stallion. "I want you to keep watch until I return."

"Me?" Squib said.

"You have a rifle. I've shown you how to use it." Fargo shoved the Sharps into the boot.

"True, but I have no experience whatsoever along these lines. Any old beast could sneak right up behind me and I'd never know it."

"Stay alert," Fargo said, bending to work on a cinch. "In the wild, a man has to learn to have eyes in the back of his head if he wants to live long."

"An anatomical impossibility," Squib said nervously. "I'd much rather you didn't go anywhere."

"Me, too," Elizabeth piped up. "Why must you leave us

alone again? After last night, I should think you would have learned your lesson."

Fargo paused. All three were gazing at him like frightened children whose teacher was about to abandon them. He wasn't ready to reveal the truth, yet neither could he ride off without warning them. "There might be hostiles in the area."

Ernest Squib shot up off the ground so fast he nearly stumbled into the fire. "Savages? Nearby? How many? What kind? Where are they?"

"I said there might be," Fargo stressed. "I won't know for sure until I've gone for a look-see." Forking leather, he pulled his hat brim low. "Don't make the fire too big," he advised. "Keep someone on watch at all times." He thought of something else. "When you're on guard, sit with your back to the stream so nothing can get at you from behind without being heard."

"An excellent suggestion," Squib said.

"Glad you approve." Fargo tapped his spurs against the pinto's flanks and galloped to the west, in order to go around the rise rather than up and over the crest where he would be silhouetted against the sky. He wound among the sparsely treed hills, the scent of sage strong in the air.

A quarter of a mile from camp, Fargo slowed to a walk. From there on he advanced in stages, going a few dozen yards at a time and then stopping to visually probe the deepening night.

A mile and a half from the basin, Fargo drew rein. The odor of wood smoke was mixed with that of the sage. Rising in the stirrups, he sniffed the breeze, swiveling right and left to pinpoint the position of the fire making the smoke. He saw no sign of it, but the smoke was coming from the southwest.

Holding the Ovaro to a walk, his Colt in hand, Fargo covered a hundred feet. In the shelter of a scrub oak he dismounted and tied the pinto.

The stretch of terrain ahead appeared flat and offered scant cover, but somewhere out there someone had a fire going. Fargo crept from concealment, the darkness a welcome shroud. The smoke was like an invisible beacon, drawing him steadily nearer its source. Presently a low nicker warned him that he was closer than he thought. Still he saw no fire, which puzzled him—until a dry wash opened up in front of him.

To the right, sixty feet off, crackled a small fire, the kind an Indian would make. A paint horse, the kind an Indian would ride, was tied to a bush. Its owner, however, was nowhere in sight.

Fargo lay on his stomach to wait the man out. More and more stars blazed in the heavens, and the wind increased, as it usually did at that time of the day. The paint stood with head hung low. The scene was so peaceful that Fargo had to fight off an urge to doze.

About twenty minutes had gone by when a shadow loomed on the other side of the wash. It had materialized out of the night as if made of air. Fargo saw it out of the corner of an eye and did not move a muscle until the shadow descended and made for the fire.

It was the half-breed, Charley Crow, a dead rabbit dangling from one hand, a bow in the other, a quiver full of arrows slanted across his back. He walked a score of feet, then stopped and surveyed the wash walls as if he suspected something was amiss.

Fargo held his breath and didn't so much as blink. A man like Charley Crow had razor-keen senses and would vanish at the first hint of a threat. Only after the breed had gone on did he exhale quietly.

Fargo had entertained the slim hope that he was wrong, that Morgan wasn't after them, that they would reach the settlements safely. But clearly Charley Crow had been sent on ahead to keep track of them until Morgan and the rest caught up. He thought of Melanie and Erica Dunn and the other boarder and elected to cut the odds by one.

Swinging parallel to the wash, Fargo crawled toward the small fire. He needed to be close when he fired, needed to be sure he didn't miss. The breed wouldn't give him a second chance.

Charley Crow had drawn his butcher knife and was peeling the rabbit's hide off. He stopped and looked up, almost directly at Fargo, who hugged the ground. After a while the breed resumed carving, but he would lift his head every so often.

Fargo imitated a turtle. He moved slowly, freezing whenever the killer raised his eyes from the rabbit. Bit by bit he narrowed the gap, and had whittled it down to less than twenty-five feet when the unforeseen took place.

A clump of brush barred Fargo's way. He snaked to the right to go on by when suddenly a spooked mouse or chipmunk dashed from the clump and on down into the wash.

Instantly Charley Crow was on his feet, a deadly shaft notched to the sinew bowstring. Unlike someone like Ernest Squib, who would have rushed toward the spot where the mouse had appeared, Charley Crow backpedaled into the darkness, blending himself into the background.

Fargo lost sight of him. Charley Crow was bound to investigate, so Fargo had to get out of there before the breed spotted him. He hurried on all fours to the right, away from the wash, moving as stealthily as the Sioux among whom he had once lived. He traveled forty feet, which he assumed was far enough, and rose on his knees.

Whizzing out of the night came a long shaft, which imbedded itself in the earth within inches of his right leg. Fargo dived to the left and rolled. He heard another arrow thud into the ground within a hand's width of his face.

The breed knew exactly where he was.

Surging into a crouch, Fargo ran for all he was worth, zigzagging to make it harder for the killer to hit him. A third arrow streaked over his shoulder. An inch lower and he would have been transfixed.

No longer having a need for stealth, Fargo exploded into an all-out run, winding across the sage with the half-breed in determined pursuit. A glance showed an inky form bounding along like an antelope to his rear.

Fargo knew it would be hard to get away. He had to slow the breed down. To that end, he abruptly halted, spun, and thumbed the pistol twice. At the second retort the form disappeared as if swallowed by the soil, but Fargo knew better. He crouched and crept to the west, using all available cover.

A couple of minutes passed without incident. Fargo was congratulating himself on getting away when an arrow nearly took off his head. Flattening, he snapped a shot in the direction the shaft had come from.

Working his elbows as if they were levers, Fargo scuttled for a dozen feet as if he were a giant lizard, never once lifting his stomach off the ground. He paused to listen and an arrow clipped his hat.

Inspiration struck. Fargo crawled another four yards, then stopped close to some sage, removed his hat, and jammed it onto a bush. Swiftly he went ten feet farther and turned. It was one of the oldest tricks around, but it just might work.

Tense seconds ticked by as Fargo waited for Charley Crow to put an arrow into the hat. He knew the breed would spot it eventually and could only hope the killer made the mistake of thinking it was still on his head.

Staying as still as the sage around him, Fargo swiveled his eyes, seeking his enemy. When several minutes had gone by, he knew something was wrong. Charley Crow wasn't going to take the bait. He wondered if the breed had seen him take the hat off, or had simply guessed the truth. Whatever the case, he had to keep going.

But first Fargo retraced his route and reached out to snatch his hat off the sage. At the sound of drumming moccasins he perceived in a flash that he was the one who had been tricked, that the clever breed had used his own trap against him. He whirled, bringing the Colt up, but he was too slow, by half, and the stocky warrior hurtled into him as if blasted from a circus cannon.

The jarring impact knocked Fargo onto his back. A vise clamped onto his right wrist as he went down and he was unable to bring the pistol to bear. At the selfsame moment, Fargo brought his left arm up and deflected a knife thrust aimed at his throat. He succeeded in wrapping his fingers around the breed's wrist.

Charley Crow hissed like a bucket of riled rattlers and strove with all his might to force the blade into Fargo's flesh. Fargo was doing the opposite, trying to tear his right arm loose so he could shoot. They struggled fiercely, rolling right and left, the sage tearing at their clothes, their faces.

Suddenly a knee rammed into Fargo's gut. His stomach tried to leap into his mouth and the world dipped and danced like a child's spinning top. He felt his left arm begin to weaken and the scrape of cold steel on his skin.

The breed was beside himself with fury. He threw all of his considerable weight and muscle into a driving thrust, a thrust

Fargo could not begin to resist. And he was too smart to try. Fargo let his arm bend with the blow and jerked his neck to the left so the flat of the blade brushed against his neck, not the razor edge, sparing himself from a lethal stab.

Instantly Fargo whipped his knee into the breed's midsection. Charley Crow was jolted but clung on. Lips wide, he tried to bite Fargo's nose off. To deter him, Fargo smashed his forehead into the killer's mouth. There was a crunch, and Charley Crow growled just like a rabid wolf.

With all their tossing and turning, Fargo wound up on his side. He pushed to his knees, even though their arms were still locked together. The breed tried to flip him off balance, but he stayed erect. For a few moments they were face to face, Charley Crow's features set in a mask of bestial hatred.

Fargo thought of Melanie and new strength pumped into his limbs. He let go of the Colt even as he wrenched his right arm loose. Then, pivoting on one knee, he grabbed the breed's knife arm with both hands, twisted sharply, shifted, and speared the killer's own knife up into Charley Crow's gut.

A startled squeal was the only sound the breed uttered. He gaped in disbelief at Fargo, then looked down at himself, at his life's blood pouring out.

Fargo held on, the blade jammed to the hilt. Charley Crow tried to pry his fingers loose. In order to hasten the inevitable, Fargo bunched his shoulder muscles and surged upward, slicing the breed open from the stomach to the sternum. The killer clutched at his innards as they oozed out but could not keep them from spilling over his fingers onto the ground. A vile stench filled the air, so vile Fargo nearly gagged.

Wrenching the knife blade out, Fargo rose and moved back a step. The breed was fading fast. Doubled over, Charley Crow trembled but made no sound.

Fargo needed answers, and although he knew he would be wasting his time, he asked, "Why did Morgan try to have me killed? Why were all those others murdered?"

The half-breed looked up, his spite as plain as ever.

"What is Morgan's link to the schoolmarm?" Fargo tried again. "How far behind you are the rest?"

Charley Crow's mouth moved. He rose higher, as if to speak, but instead let fly with spit aimed at Fargo's face. It fell short, onto the tip of Fargo's boot. "With my dying breath, I curse you, white-eye! I hope the others kill you! I hope they make you suffer!" He would have gone on had the end not dawned. Gasping and shaking, he made one determined effort to stand, but his legs buckled and he pitched onto his chest and was still.

"Good riddance, bastard," Fargo growled.

Recovering his Colt and his hat, Fargo wiped the butcher knife clean on the renegade's leggings and stripped off the beaded sheath. The only other item the breed had on him was a small piece of rose quartz suspended from a rawhide thong around his neck. Why the man had seen fit to wear it, Fargo had no idea. He left it on.

Next Fargo dragged the body to the fire and arranged things so that Charley Crow appeared to be sleeping under a blanket. He took hold of the paint by its bridle and led it to the Ovaro. Mounting, he headed north.

One down and five to go, Fargo reflected, unless Frederick Morgan was along, in which case he would be up against an even half dozen. He'd faced stiffer odds, but not very often.

Fargo took his sweet time returning. He was in no hurry to be pestered silly by pointless questions from the schoolmarms and Squib. It was close to midnight when he reached the rim of the basin and saw reddish orange flames below. Two figures were spread out beside the fire. A third was huddled in a blanket.

The paint behaved itself until Fargo reined up in front of the string. Then it stamped and balked, unwilling to be tied with the rest of the stock. Fargo gave it no choice. As he strolled toward the fire, he saw Elizabeth Langtree's lovely features framed by the blanket. It figured. His luck was running true to form.

"Welcome back," she whispered. "We were all terribly worried."

"Any coffee left?" Fargo asked.

"Plenty. Help yourself." Elizabeth glanced at the paint. "Where did that come from?"

"I found it," Fargo lied. "Must have strayed off from an Indian village.

"How convenient," the schoolmarm said, but she did not

press the issue. Holding out a tin cup, she said, "Pour some for me, handsome, if you would be so kind."

Fargo did, and sat down. Felicia and Squib were both sound asleep, the schoolmaster snoring loud enough to rouse the dead. "Whose turn is it to stand guard next?"

"Felicia's, but not for another two hours," Elizabeth answered, her cherry lips curving upward. "Why? What did you have in mind?"

"I was just asking," Fargo said. He surveyed the area. "Did you hear anything while I was gone, or see anything out of the ordinary?"

"Ernest thought he saw a skunk over by the stream and about laid an egg. All we heard were coyotes and wolves and owls. Just like last night and the night before."

"Good," Fargo said. He was convinced that Morgan and company were a full day or more away, which gave him time to come up with a plan. Taking his cup with him, he rose to make a circuit of the camp before turning in. As he passed Felicia Taugner he thought he saw her eyes snap shut, but when he turned and stared at her, she seemed to be asleep.

At the stream, Fargo washed his hands. He'd noticed while drinking his coffee that he had blood on his fingers. The water was cold to the touch. He applied a handful to his neck and shoulders.

"Too bad it's not deeper. We could go for a swim."

Fargo had not heard Elizabeth walk up. That made twice she had been able to get close to him without his noticing, a feat few had ever done. "What do you do? Walk on air?" he remarked, and stood to go on by her. Her warm hand fell on his own, stopping him.

"Why do you treat me the way you do? I know men who would leap at the chance to be alone with me in the dark."

"I need to turn in," Fargo said.

"What's your rush?" Elizabeth responded, sliding her full body next to his. Her hair shimmered in the pale glow from the fire, and her eyes sparkled with raw passion.

"We shouldn't," Fargo said.

"Why the hell not? Are you thinking of becoming a monk or something? Don't you like women?"

"I like them just fine."

"You could have fooled me," Elizabeth mocked him, moving her face so close she eclipsed everything else. "Either you're the shyest son of a gun who ever lived, or you suffered a brain injury when you were a kid. Which is it?"

"Neither," Fargo said. He made one last attempt to leave, but she held on and contrived to mold her body to his. Her breasts jutted against his arm and chest, her thighs were like smooth marble against the back of his hand.

"So what will it be?" Elizabeth teased. "Would you rather hug me or an empty blanket?" The tip of her tongue swirled around the edge of her lips. "Are you man enough to make the right choice?"

Fargo had tried, really, really tried. Short of slugging her on the jaw, he had done all in his power to persuade her he wasn't interested. It wasn't his fault that she refused to take no for an answer. And it wasn't his fault that he was, after all, only human.

Elizabeth let out a soft moan when Fargo suddenly covered her twin mounds with his hands and squeezed hard. She was caught by surprise, and arched her back. Her face tilted up toward him. Like a bird of prey swooping in for the kill, Fargo smothered her yielding mouth with his and darted his tongue between her parted teeth.

It took a few seconds for the schoolmarm to recover and respond. Fargo felt her hands on his buttocks. He ground into her, his hard organ stroking the junction of her legs. Her lips were glued to his and she panted heavily through her nose.

Fargo showed no mercy. Dropping his right hand down low, he abruptly slid it between her thighs and grabbed her womanhood. Elizabeth quivered and drew back, overcome.

"Oh. Oh, my word."

"Does this answer your question?" Fargo said gruffly, then forced himself to release her and walk on past. A gnawing ache in his loins made him wish he had carried her off into the night to do as he pleased. But he couldn't, not yet, not until he knew which side she was on. Spreading out his blanket, he reclined, turning his back to her so she wouldn't see the bulge in his pants. The sweet taste of her lingered in his mouth, driving him crazy with desire.

It took Fargo a long time to fall asleep.

10

The next morning started off cloudy. A bank of roiling clouds crowned the Rockies, promising heavy rain before the day was done unless the wind shifted and carried the storm to the south.

Fargo loaded their supplies onto the pack animals, helped by Ernest Squib. The teacher had been bending over backwards to do all he could around the camp; he'd lent a hand watering the stock and volunteered to put out the fire. Now, listening to Squib hum while he worked, Fargo commented, "You're in fine spirits today."

"It's this wonderful climate," Ernest replied, beaming. "Haven't you noticed? I'm not sniffling anymore. The dust and the grass don't bother me nearly as much as they did before. I think your cure is working."

"Glad to hear it," Fargo said. The wilderness had a way of toughening people whether they wanted to toughen up or not.

"Yes, sir," Squib went on. "Give me another six months and I might give up teaching to become a mountain man. I can see myself now, living in a rustic cabin high in the mountains, killing game for my meals and making my clothes from animal hides. It would be glorious!"

"I think you're getting a little ahead of yourself," Fargo said. "Before a person goes jumping into a deep lake, he should first learn how to swim."

"How quaint," Squib said, and inhaled deeply. "Smell that air! It's like a bouquet of flowers. And to think I was all set to go off to Europe and live in a musty old castle."

Fargo finished tying a knot. "You wanted to go teach over there?"

Squib shrugged. "Or whatever would keep food on the

table. I've long dreamt of traveling to Europe, ever since reading *Ivanhoe* when I was younger. Sir Walter Scott was the finest writer who ever lived, in my opinion." He paused. "Have you read any of his works?"

"Not lately," Fargo said with a straight face.

"Too bad. You really should. He had a tremendous influence on James Fenimore Cooper, you know. Have you read any of Cooper's works?"

"Can't say as I have."

"What do you like to read, then?"

"Tracks," Fargo said, and walked off before he hurt the man's feelings by laughing aloud at Squib's comical expression.

Soon they were on the move again, Squib eagerly taking up his position at the end of the line behind the paint, which Fargo had added to the string of packhorses. They climbed higher into the hills, passing the Cache la Poudre river well before noon.

Fargo pressed on until the middle of the day, when he stopped at a small spring to give the animals a breather. He walked to an open spot and studied the rolling landscape they had covered for sign of pursuit. This time he heard Elizabeth Langtree walking toward him and turned. She had been giving him mischievous looks all morning, grinning and winking as if they shared a personal secret. "Sometime tomorrow we'll strike open country," he revealed.

"Oh?" she responded, not sounding the least bit interested. Placing her hands on her hips, she grinned, then puckered those incredible lips of hers and blew him a kiss. "I had a hard time getting to sleep last night, big man. How about you?"

"Slept like a baby," Fargo fibbed.

"Oh?" Elizabeth sounded disappointed. "Are you telling me that you weren't the least bit aroused by what we did?"

"It was nothing special," Fargo said, relishing the chance to give her a taste of her own medicine. It tickled him when she angrily stamped a foot.

"I had no idea you could be so rude," Elizabeth declared. "And I don't like having my interest in someone thrown back in my face like a dirty towel. If you don't watch yourself, mister, it will be a cold day in hell before you get your hands on my body again."

Deliberately, Fargo yawned.

Elizabeth Langtree looked fit to be tied. Spinning, she stormed off.

Fargo wasn't fooled. She would be back. She was toying with him, playing a game that some women liked to play, trying to make him feel guilty so she could wrap him around her finger. It was a bunch of silly nonsense he knew all too well and had no time for.

Someone else came toward him. It was Felicia Taugner, as primly dressed as ever, and she did not appear very happy. "Mr. Fargo, I would like to have a word with you," she announced crisply.

"What about?" Fargo asked, even though he had already guessed.

"Your behavior, sir. I must say that I find your conduct totally without merit. When I was told that you were the best scout around, I had no idea you were also prone to taking advantage of those who hire you."

Fargo resented the accusation. "I haven't taken advantage of anyone."

"Then how would you describe your behavior last night with regard to Miss Langtree?"

"You tell me, lady," Fargo said. "I know you were awake the whole time. If you thought I was out of line, why didn't you speak up then? Or did it get you all excited?"

Felicia blushed. "I never! How dare you!"

"One other thing," Fargo said. "Since you were watching, you know that Miss Langtree was the one who threw herself at me. Maybe you should be having this talk with her instead." When she made no reply, he knew that she agreed. "It seems to me that schoolmarms shouldn't go around rubbing up against every man that strikes their fancy, but maybe I'm wrong."

"No, you're absolutely right," Felicia said. "We have a duty to live by high standards in order to inspire the young minds we mold." She paused. "I will confess that Miss Langtree's actions trouble me. She is unlike any teacher I have ever known.

Every time I try to discuss our line of work, she changes the subject."

"Maybe she should give up teaching and get a job in a saloon."

"Mr. Fargo!" Felicia said. Then, despite herself, she laughed. "I suppose she does have the right temperament for the job."

"Not to mention the body," Fargo said, and was pleased when Miss Taugner laughed louder. When she let her hair down, so to speak, she could be quite pleasant. He had to admit that he liked her. She had always treated him with respect, and never did anything that would smear her good standing as a schoolmarm. It was too bad, he mused, that she might be hiding something.

"You are a card, Mr. Fargo," Felicia said. She gazed toward the horses and turned serious. "That paint you brought back?"

"What about it?"

"Did you really find it wandering these hills? I can't help but think of that incident in the Imperial. And this whole trip you've been acting as if you expect someone to jump out at you any given minute of the day." Felicia locked her pretty eyes on his. "I want the truth, sir. Is there something you're not telling us? Are we in any kind of danger?"

Fargo did not answer right away. She sounded so sincere, acted so innocent, that he found it hard to believe she had led anything other than a life of virtue. He decided to seize the bull by the horns. Her reaction alone might tell him something. "Do you know a man named Frederick Morgan?"

Felicia never batted an eye. She shook her head, saying, "No, I can't say as I do. Who is he?"

If she was putting on an act, she deserved to be on the stage in New York City, Fargo mused. "Someone with an unhealthy interest in you and your friends. He hired the man I tried to catch at your hotel, scum by the name of Dixie Lee. Later, that same man and another tried to pry information from me. They wanted to know how much you knew—"

"About what?" Felicia cut in, appearing genuinely stunned. "I've never met anyone called Dixie in my whole life."

"There's more," Fargo said. Since he had let the cat out of the bag, he figured he might as well reveal everything.

"Morgan has hired a bunch of killers besides Lee. They butchered three people in Denver, one of them a good friend of mine."

"How awful!" Felicia said, her face betraying shock. "Why would they do such a thing?"

"If I knew that, I'd be a happy man." Fargo pointed at the paint. "That cayuse belonged to a half-breed butcher called Charley·Crow. I caught him on our back trail and he tried to kill me."

Felicia clasped her hands at her waist. "And you killed him? Oh, my word! I don't know what to say. Believe me, Mr. Fargo, when I tell you that I don't have the slightest idea what any of this is all about."

"I do believe you, ma'am," Fargo said. And he did. Learning to read people was as essential to surviving in the wild as learning to read tracks, and he was better than a fair hand at both. But her honesty only made the situation more puzzling than ever. What possible link could there be between Morgan and her?

The next moment a blast of chill wind howled past them, reminding Fargo of the gathering storm. The clouds were bearing down on them like a herd of stampeded buffalo. In less than five minutes, nature would unleash its full fury on the foothills.

"We need to find some cover," Fargo said, nodding at a stand of pines forty yards to the west. "Tell the others." He ran toward the packhorses, which were fidgeting, and got hold of the lead rope. As he swung onto the Ovaro, the teachers scrambled to their own mounts.

Fargo led them toward the pines at a trot. Lightning rent the sky a few miles away, attended by the rumbling boom of thunder. As Fargo well knew, storms in the West made storms east of the Mississippi seem like weak sisters in comparison. The winds were much stronger, the rain much heavier. Mere words could not do the raging elements justice. The teachers were in for an experience they would never forget.

Heavy raindrops began to splatter down as Fargo reached the stand. Sliding from the saddle, he ushered the packhorses into the pines and tied each and every one to a different tree.

The teachers followed his lead—Ernest Squib grinning like an idiot, Elizabeth and Felicia appearing slightly worried.

There was a brief lull. The wind died, the rain slackened. "Maybe it will pass us by," Elizabeth said.

Fargo knew better. He was the only one who didn't flinch when the wind intensified with a vengeance, shrieking and wailing like a demented banshee as it tore through the trees. Many of the pines were bent low. Several cracked with loud retorts that mimicked the firing of a shotgun. Some of the pack animals nickered in fright and tried to break loose.

For the next several minutes, Fargo was kept so busy calming the horses he had little time for anything else. The storm struck in all its primal wrath, the wind so strong it could bowl a person over if he wasn't careful, the rain so heavy that the teachers were drenched to the bone in the span of seconds.

Fargo heard Ernest Squib laugh with excitement. The greenhorn failed to realize the danger they were in. Lightning crackled in the heavens without cease, and at any moment a bolt might strike one of the pines.

Suddenly one did, hitting a tree at the edge of the stand. The brilliant flash and concussion set the horses to rearing and plunging, and it was all Fargo could do to keep them from bolting. When at last he had them calmed down, he looked around and discovered Felicia Taugner on the ground.

Dashing to her side, Fargo scooped her into his arms and carried her over to where he had been. Elizabeth and Ernest were huddled under a nearby tree, Squib no longer beaming childishly.

Fargo gently set Felicia down. She was unharmed, as near as he could tell. She had been the closest to the bolt, so either the shock of the blast had felled her or she had simply fainted. She blinked a few times, then she sat up, crying, "The lightning!"

"You're all right," Fargo assured her, giving her arm a squeeze. "Stay low until the storm has gone on by." He saw her nod, then she did the unexpected—she threw herself into his arms and clung to him, trembling uncontrollably.

Fargo didn't know what to do. The pack animals were still acting up, but he didn't want to shove her aside when she needed comforting. He compromised and held her close while keeping one eye on the horses.

For minutes on end nature whipped the earth. Thunder beat in a steady cadence. The wind screamed down off the mountains and out across the plains.

The first to sense the storm had passed its peak was Fargo. He said as much in Felicia's ear and she nodded. Her warm breath fanned his neck every time she breathed, and the intimate feel of her body against his made his loins stir. It surprised him to learn her prudish style of clothing concealed a figure every bit as shapely as that of Elizabeth Langtree's.

At length the rain slackened to a drizzle and the wind died to a stiff breeze. Fargo rose, Felicia still clinging to him. She glanced up sheepishly, coughed, and quickly dropped her arms.

"I'm sorry. I didn't mean to act so foolishly."

"You didn't," Fargo said, patting her hand. She made no attempt to pull it away. And there was a new look in her eyes, a certain curiosity Fargo had seen before in the eyes of other women. He knew what it meant, and he smiled.

Out from under the pine came Squib and Langtree. His wet clothes hung on his frame like discards on a scarecrow. Her hair was plastered to her head, the back of her dress a mess where she had leaned against the trunk.

"Look at me! I may never dry out!" Elizabeth complained, brushing at a sap stain. Her large breasts were clearly outlined by the wet fabric, and Fargo could see them jiggle as she moved.

"We need to build a fire before I catch my death of pneumonia," the schoolmaster said.

Fargo sighed. So much for the new, tough Ernest Squib. "What would we build a fire with?" he responded. "Every piece of wood within five miles is as soaked as you are. We'll push on until evening. By then we should be out of the area drenched by the thunderstorm."

"You hope," Elizabeth muttered.

It was a depressed party of travelers that Fargo guided on

out of the pines, all except for Felicia Taugner. She wore a steady smile for the first time since Fargo had met her, and every so often she cast shy glances at him, admiring him on the sly.

Fargo had other things on his mind. The storm had delayed them much too long, a delay that could prove costly if it hadn't also slowed down Morgan's pack. He figured that by now Charley Crow's body had been found. Morgan was crafty enough to put two and two together, and might push on rapidly to overtake them.

Once the sun dipped toward the horizon, Fargo kept his eyes peeled for a likely spot to make camp, a spot with forage and water. It would be all the better if it was a place they could defend if attacked. Under no circumstances could he afford to make camp in open country.

The terrain favored them. They wound down through smaller and smaller hills toward verdant country bordering the Medicine Bow Mountains. In a gully rimmed by trees and boulders, Fargo called a halt. There was only one way in or out, which would work in their favor if they were attacked. The only drawback was that riflemen posted on the rims could pin them down, maybe wipe them out.

After the horses had been tended and a fire made, Fargo picked up the Sharps. "You'll have to make do with coffee and jerky for your supper," he told the teachers. "Keep the fire small and don't sleep too close to it."

"Where the devil are you off to this time?" Squib inquired.

"Up high, to keep watch," Fargo said. "I won't be back until morning, so don't wait up for me."

Elizabeth Langtree frowned. "If I didn't know better, I'd swear you can't stand the sight of us. Whenever we stop, you always have somewhere to go."

Felicia surprised them by speaking up for him. "Don't give Skye such a hard time. He knows what he's doing. I wouldn't have hired him if he didn't."

Fargo smiled at her, then hiked toward the mouth of the gully. A steep grade brought him to the rim, where he prowled until he located a suitable niche in which to take cover. With a boulder to his back, another to his right, and thick trees to his left, he was well hidden. He settled down to wait, pulling a piece of jerky from his pocket.

The murmur of voices wafted up out of the gully, the words too faint for Fargo to make sense of what was being said. The woods were alive with crickets, and to the north a bird chirped wildly, as if in the clutches of a predator.

Fargo braced himself against the boulder behind him and re-signed himself to a long night. He spent his time trying to make sense of the whole affair, but after several hours was no closer to the answer than he had been when he started. Only one person could provide the missing pieces to the puzzle, and that was Frederick Morgan.

The voices below died off. Fargo looked down and saw them turning in. Most of the horses were dozing, including his Ovaro. All appeared peaceful, but as he had learned the hard way, in the wild appearances could be deceiving.

It must have been ten minutes later that the breeze brought him the sound of feet knocking dirt and gravel loose on the steep grade. Fargo ducked low and tucked the Sharps to his shoulder. From where he sat, he could see anyone coming over the crest. Sure enough, moments later a dark figure appeared, but immediately he could tell that it was not one of Morgan's men. Long hair flowed in the wind, as did the hem of a dress.

"Elizabeth!" Fargo snapped. "What the hell are you doing up here?"

"It's me, Skye. Felicia," came the timid reply.

A feather could have floored Fargo. He straightened as she meekly advanced. "Is something wrong?"

"No. Not at all," Felicia answered softly. "I just wanted to talk to you, is all." She bit her lower lip. "But if I'm bothering you, I'll go. I wouldn't want to have you be upset with me."

Fargo had another choice to make. If he told her to leave, she might take it hard. She was just beginning to have confidence in herself and needed to be encouraged, not told to get lost. "I can spare a few minutes," he said, hoping that he wasn't making a mistake that would get all of them killed.

Felicia grinned shyly and stepped into the narrow space between the boulders. There was barely room for her, and when she faced him, her chest was a finger's width from his own. Being small, she had to crane her neck to look up at him.

"Thank you. I can use some nice conversation after the spat I had with Elizabeth."

"I heard an argument," Fargo mentioned.

"Ernest and I were talking about teaching. He brought up that it's hard to deal with children who like to give teachers a hard time for the mere sake of causing trouble. Elizabeth said that she thinks those who act up should be caned. She even claimed that at the last school she worked at, caning was standard. But I know better. She most recently taught in Philadelphia, and they have banned caning there."

"Maybe some still practice it," Fargo said, unable to see what the fuss was about when most of the parents in the country believed the best way to discipline a problem child was with a trip to the woodshed.

"I suppose," Felicia said, and fiddled with her high collar. "But I really don't care to talk about her. She and I have nothing in common. Which is strange. From her letters, I had the idea we were a lot alike."

Fargo leaned the Sharps against the boulder. "What about Squib?"

"Oh, he's a gentleman. The funny thing is, I understand that he never wanted to take the job at first. He saw the ad but laughed it off. To his way of thinking, no one in their right mind would want to live on the frontier." Felicia gazed into the gully. "I don't know why he changed his mind. Now that he has, he swears he may never leave this part of the country. He thinks he can make something of himself."

Fargo suspected that she was talking for the sake of hearing herself talk, that she was as skittish as a month-old colt and deathly afraid of what he might do. Moving forward a fraction, he asked. "What about you?"

"How do you mean?"

"What are your plans?"

"To go on teaching. Maybe one day I'll find a husband and raise a brood of my own." She studied him. "By any chance are you looking for a wife?"

"I won't lie to you," Fargo said. "I'm not the marrying kind. If a husband is all you want, you'd better go on back down."

Felicia licked her lips and shifted her weight from one foot to another. "Some men would have lied just to get what they

113

wanted. But not you. For all your rough ways, you're an honest, dependable man, the kind a woman can turn to when she's in need. I respect you for that, Skye."

At last she had gotten to the point. "In need how, exactly?" Fargo asked.

The schoolmarm's answer wasn't in words. She abruptly pressed herself against him and placed her dainty hands on his wide shoulders. Pulling his face down to hers, she melted her hot lips against his.

11

Skye Fargo responded to Felicia Taugner's kiss by cupping her bottom and grinding into her. His ardor matched hers. But inwardly, he questioned his judgment.

It never failed. Women had an uncanny knack for picking the worst possible moment to wax romantic. There they were, trying to reach the settlements before they were jumped by the vilest pack of sadistic killers who ever lived, and the schoolmarm wanted to make love!

Fargo knew he should push her away and order her to leave. He knew that by giving his lust free rein he was tempting fate. But for the life of him, he couldn't help himself. Her lips tasted so sweet, her breath was so sugary, her breasts so soft and full, that he couldn't bring himself to do anything other than what he did—namely, give her a kiss the likes of which she would remember all her born days.

"Oh, my!" Felicia breathed when they broke for air. "I had no idea! I feel like a volcano inside."

"And we're just starting," Fargo said, before bending his mouth to hers a second time. She met his tongue halfway, hers circling his again and again. All the while she rubbed herself against him, her small form dwarfed by his much larger frame.

Fargo slid a hand between them to massage her right breast. At the first contact, Felicia moaned and thrust her hips into him with vigor. When he lowered his left hand to her other breast, it triggered a reaction he would never have anticipated. She went berserk with passion, kissing and sucking and licking while roving her hands over every square inch of his body that she could reach. It was as if an inner dam had burst, releasing all the sexual hunger she had pent up over the years, and she was determined to eat him alive to make up for lost time.

Fargo could not get over how sweet she tasted. He wondered if she had swallowed some sugar before coming to see him. Each kiss was like tasting delicious candy. He could not get enough of her.

Apparently Felicia felt the same way. She glued her mouth to his. Her hands, always in motion, roved steadily lower and lower.

It was another shock to Fargo when she suddenly slid a palm onto his iron-hard manhood. His throat constricted, and he swore he could hear his blood rushing through his veins.

"So big!" Felicia cooed. "I didn't realize."

"Here. Take a look," Fargo said, and swiftly unbuckled his gun belt and his belt. All it took was a deft jerk of his wrist and his pants were down around his knees. She stood as still as a statue while he took hold of her wrist and placed her fingers on his pole.

"It's so smooth, like marble," Felicia said.

Fargo bent to unbutton her dress, his fingers flying in his eagerness to see her naked. She stroked him as he worked, her eyelids hooded, her body swaying suggestively. His shirt joined her dress on the ground. At long last Fargo saw how magnificent her body truly was, and it made his mouth water.

Pressing his mouth onto her right nipple, Fargo swirled the tip with his tongue. His right hand delved between her silken legs and lightly brushed the core of her being. She quivered, her thighs exquisite in the starlight, the picture of ecstasy.

"There's something I want to do," Felicia said huskily. "I hope you won't mind."

"Do?" Fargo said, not having the slightest idea what she meant. He found out, though, when her mouth closed on his member. A ripple of pure pleasure coursed down his spine. He threw back his head and sucked in the cool night air while she did something similar below his waist.

Fargo had a wildcat on his hands. Felicia seemed to want to explore him from head to toe. Whatever her hands didn't touch, her lips did. She inflamed him, filled him with a carnal thirst only one thing could quench.

Presently Fargo picked her up, took a few steps away from

the boulders, and set her down on a patch of grass. She played with his ear, lathered his throat, rubbed the small of his back. He devoted himself to her gorgeous globes for the better part of five minutes, and when he was done her chest was heaving like a bellows.

"More, Skye. I want more."

Fargo did his best to oblige her. His mouth traced a path from between her firm breasts across her flat stomach to the junction of her legs. A heady scent made him giddy with desire. When he slid lower, she cried out and gripped his hair. At the initial stroke of his tongue, Felicia started bucking like a mustang, forcing him to hold tight onto her hips to keep her in place.

"Oh! Oh! Oh!" she exclaimed. "I never knew it could be like this!"

Her next sound was a sharp intake of breath as Fargo buried his tongue inside of her. To his amazement, she tasted just as sweet as she had higher up. He drove her into a frenzy by rubbing the tip of his tongue over her tiny pleasure knob. She wrapped both legs around his waist and clamped tight while at the same time she entwined her hands in his hair and mashed his face hard into her inner well.

Fargo slaked his thirst, and then some. He kept on licking until she was kicking in abandon and begging him to consummate their union. At the slightest pressure she thrashed and squirmed, as highly strung as the finest violin, ready to play a serenade of love.

"Please," Felicia pleaded. "Please don't make me wait any longer."

Easing up onto his knees, Fargo positioned himself on top of her, inserted the head of his organ into her, and, gripping her breasts, rammed inside to the hilt. To his consternation, he met an obstruction. So swiftly did it happen that he had pierced through to her inner core before he quite realized the significance. "You're not—," he blurted.

"I was," Felicia said.

The clues had been staring Fargo right in the face. He held himself still a few moments, gathering his wits. All of a sudden he saw her prim conduct in a whole new light. It was important that he treat her with special care. Instead of slamming into her as he had wanted, he stroked lightly, smoothly, letting the intensity build slowly instead of exploding all at once.

Felicia clung to Fargo, her eyes limpid pools of sheer ecstasy, her sleek body caked with perspiration. She matched his thrusts, force for force, her silken sheath wrapping around his rigid sword as if the pair were made for each other.

Meanwhile, Fargo kissed her lips, her breasts, her throat. She was incredibly hot to the touch, especially her nipples and her inner thighs. Her fingernails raked his shoulders, his upper back.

A great deal of time went by. Fargo was in superb control of himself and in no rush to get their lovemaking over with. He savored every moment, stoking the fires deep within him, pacing himself for the explosion to come.

Felicia was adrift in sexual delirium. She wore a look of utter contentment as her velvety body rose to meet his every stroke. For one so tiny, she had muscles of steel. She showed no signs of tiring, even after half an hour.

It was much, much later that Fargo felt her inner walls convulse. She looped her arms around his neck and hung on for dear life while her hips went wild of their own accord. Her backside worked like a pumphandle, driving up into him in a measured tempo. At long last she was climaxing, and Fargo let her do so until she drained her juices and sagged back onto the ground, spent and exhausted.

"It's not over yet," Fargo warned her, increasing the urgency of his thrust. Her lovely eyes widened, then narrowed, and she grinned happily. Fargo pounded into her again and again, his hands on her hips, their two bodies as one. He encircled a hard nipple with his mouth as the impending explosion built to the critical point at the base of his pole.

When it came, it was like the end of the world. A sensation like a red-hot knife seared through Fargo's body, but a knife that produced supreme delight, not pain. Pinwheels of flashing light flared before his eyes. For that instant in time, nothing else mattered except the pure rapture of his release. He kept on pumping, coasting slower and slower until he was totally spent.

For a few minutes they lay there, damp skin on damp skin.

Fargo felt her shift to make herself more comfortable, and rose onto his elbows to spare her the burden of his weight.

Felicia smiled nervously, then pecked his chin. "Was it all right for you?"

"Need you ask?" Fargo said.

"I did like I should, then? Everything was as it should be?"

Some men would have laughed at the worry in her eyes, but not Fargo. "You did just fine," he assured her.

"I did, didn't I?" Giggling, Felicia closed her eyes and sighed with contentment. "I feel so tired all of a sudden."

"You're not the only one," Fargo said, sliding to the right to lie beside her. Cradling her head on his shoulder, he allowed himself to drift off, confident he would wake up in a very short while.

But he was wrong.

The instant Fargo opened his eyes, he knew he had blundered badly. His lack of a good night's sleep over the past several days had finally caught up with him. A rosy band of pale light framed the eastern horizon, heralding the dawn, which was not more than an hour off.

Rising onto an elbow, Fargo listened to sparrows and robins chirp merrily in the nearby trees. He quickly dressed, then gave Felicia's elbow a gentle shake. Her eyes opened sluggishly and she stared dreamily at his face.

"What is it, my wonderful prince?"

"Morning," Fargo said, holding out her clothes.

Felicia sat up and gazed around in bewilderment. "We slept the whole night through? My word! What will the others think if they find out I didn't use my bedroll?"

Fargo stepped to the rim to give her some privacy. The camp was quiet, the horses stirring but the two teachers still sleeping soundly. When a hand closed on his wrist, he turned.

"I must have set a new record getting dressed," Felicia said. She glanced at the sleepers, then rose on her toes to kiss him. "Thank you so much for our moment together. It means more to me than you will ever know."

"We'd better go down and get a fire started," Fargo proposed before she became too sentimental. He let her go first, taking her hand when they reached the grade so he could assist her to the bottom.

Felicia hurried from there on, pulling him along. As they neared the two prone forms, she yanked her hand free and darted to her bedroll. She had just knelt beside it when Elizabeth Langtree woke up and saw her.

"My, my. Aren't you the early bird today," the raven-maned beauty said.

"Skye wants us to get an early start," Felicia responded.

Elizabeth looked around and spotted Fargo. "So there you are," she said with a smirk. "I trust you had a wonderful night up there all by yourself?"

"I made do," Fargo said, unable to tell if she was being sarcastic or not. Had she spied on them? he wondered. Did she know what had happened? Ignoring her, he set about preparing their breakfast, which consisted of coffee, pemmican, and biscuits he whipped up from scratch. The aroma of the food brought Ernest Squib out of dreamland.

"Morning, all. I'm so hungry I could eat a buffalo."

"We might see some today," Fargo disclosed.

"Really? I hope so," Squib said. "I've been disappointed in not seeing any of the big brutes sooner. Oh, I saw a few during the long stage ride west, but they were always too far off to note much detail."

"The bigger herds are well to the east of Denver at this time of year," Fargo said. "If we're lucky, we'll come on some stragglers and be able to shoot a cow. By smoking the meat, we'll have enough to last us the rest of the trip." He sipped his scalding coffee and felt it warm his insides.

"Eat jerked buffalo meat?" Elizabeth said. "The idea isn't very appealing. I'm partial to well-done steak, myself. Or seafood. I do so like lobster. Too bad I can't find any in this godforsaken country."

"We have lobsters of a sort," Fargo quipped. "Only out here we call them crayfish."

Elizabeth scrunched up her nose. "I wouldn't eat one if you paid me."

Within half an hour they were ready to leave. Fargo waited while the others mounted, then stepped into the stirrups and headed on up out of the gully. Felicia gave him a sly, warm smile, which he returned. The rest of the journey promised to be much more enjoyable than the first few days, he reflected, provided they all lived through whatever Frederick Morgan had in store for them.

Fargo no sooner had the thought than he found out. The mouth of the gully was a bottleneck with sheer slopes, allowing only one horse to go through at a time. Growing out of the right-hand slope was a pine tree. Opposite it was a cluster of boulders. Fargo was passing between them when he heard a swishing sound. Felicia screamed a warning, but too late. Before he could do so much as blink, a coil of rope fell around his shoulders.

Automatically Fargo tried to shrug the rope off while spurring the Ovaro into a gallop. His spurs were effective but the shrug was not. He left the saddle as if hurled by a catapult and smashed down onto his back in the middle of the trail.

Someone else shouted. Fargo rolled to his side and pushed to his knees, which was hard to do with his arms pinned to his side. He made a grab for the Colt, a grab that fell short when pain exploded in his ribs. Someone had kicked him. The blow knocked him down.

"Don't try that again, you slippery coon. Not if you care to go on breathing a little longer."

Fargo looked up into the barrel of a cocked Remington revolver. Above it loomed the cruel face of Eric Graven. "I knew you'd be along sometime," he said.

"Then you should have kept your eyes skinned better than you did," the mountain man said. "You're plumb careless. I expected better of the man they call the Trailsman."

Another man appeared, beside the tree. It was the lanky cowboy, who rolled up his rope as he advanced. "Howdy, mister," he said with a pronounced drawl. "The handle is Benteen. I hail from Texas, and some folks say I'm the best hand with a rope this side of the Rio Grande."

Graven spat. "Quit bragging on yourself and let's get on with this, you blamed cowpoke. I swear, I've never met anyone so in love with himself as you are."

Fargo was shoved flat and covered by the Remington while the Texan stripped off the lariat. He glanced at the teachers. Ernest Squib had the look of a small boy caught with a hand in the cookie jar, while Felicia appeared terrified. Elizabeth, oddly enough, was the only one who had stayed calm.

It was Graven who deprived Fargo of the Colt. "I'll just hold onto this hog leg of yours, mister. We wouldn't want you to have an accident."

"Not before Mr. Morgan has a talk with you, at any rate," Benteen said. "You have no idea how much he has been lookin' forward to seein' you again."

Felicia found her voice. "See here! What is the meaning of this outrage? You have no right to be treating our guide in this uncivilized manner."

Graven cackled. "Lordy, ain't you a caution! I hate to be the one to break the bad news to you, ma'am, but in these parts a man can do as he damn well pleases. Rights have nothing to do with it."

Benteen was staring at Squib. "Look at him, Eric. Sittin' on his hoss not sayin' a word, actin' like he doesn't have a care in the world."

"Cocky little bastard," Graven agreed. "Mr. Morgan will set him straight, I reckon."

Fargo was able to sit up. He made no attempt to jump his attackers. For the moment they had the upper hand. But neither had bothered to check his boots for hidden weapons.

Felicia had turned toward Ernest. "What do they mean? Do you know these horrible men?"

"I never set eyes on them before," Squib said. "And I have no idea what they are talking about."

Benteen coiled the last of his rope. "Like hell you don't, partner. Mr. Morgan told us some about you. So don't act so high and mighty around us, when we know you're no better than we are."

"Go to hell, cowboy," Squib rasped.

The Texan casually strolled over to the schoolmaster's horse, casually looked up at him and smiled, then just as casually hauled off and lashed Squib across the face with the lariat. The teacher rocked in the saddle, bloody welts marking his cheek. "I'd be obliged if you don't insult me again." Benteen said. "It wouldn't do to rile me. Mr. Morgan wants you alive, but he never said we couldn't cuff you around some if you don't behave."

Graven roared and slapped his leg. "I sure do like you, Tex.

You're a man after my own heart. You don't take a lick of guff."

"Never have, never will," Benteen boasted. "Now what say we get this outfit on the trail. If we push, we can rejoin the others by this afternoon."

Fargo rose when the mountain man gestured. The cowboy took the Sharps from the boot, and Fargo was told to climb on the stallion. He did so slowly, aware that any false move would result in his being shot. "What does Squib have to do with this?" he probed.

"You'll have to ask Morgan," Benteen said. "We don't have all the details yet. Let's just say he's a sneaky little varmint who likes to take things that don't belong to him."

"That's a damned lie!" Squib declared, forgetting himself, much to his regret. The Texan was on him in two strides, and this time the rope caught him flush on the mouth.

"What did I just tell you, boy?" Benteen said. "Do I have to take a club to your head before I can get it through your thick skull? The next time you insult me, I think I'll ask Graven here to cut off one of your toes with that big pigsticker of his. It would please me to hear you squeal like a stuck hog."

Fargo noticed that so far the killers had not paid any attention to Elizabeth and chalked it up to the fact that she had been smart enough to keep her mouth shut for once. The mountain man came around in front of him, that Remington trained squarely on his chest.

"You sit tight, there, mister, while Tex fetches our horses."

The cowboy hastened off. Only then did Fargo realize that Benteen wasn't armed with a pistol, just like back at the hotel. In all his travels, Fargo had never yet met a Texan who did not go around well-heeled. One tall tale had it that Texan fathers were fond of strapping six-shooters on their sons before the sprouts outgrew the crib stage. For Benteen to be without a pistol was akin to a bear not having hair or a cougar its claws. Fargo was sure the man had one somewhere on his person.

"What do you intend to do with us?" Felicia demanded.

"Haven't you been listening, lady?" Graven said. "We're fixing to take you to meet the man who hired us."

"And then?"

"Oh, I'd imagine that Squib, there, is going to have a lot to answer for."

"What about the rest of us?" Felicia asked.

The mountain man scratched his red beard. "Fargo will likely be meeting his Maker. I couldn't say about you. Me, all I do is as I'm told. And Benteen and me were told to take the three of you to meet our boss. That's all."

Fargo's curiosity got the better of him. "Why didn't Morgan tag along?"

Graven reached into a pocket, pulled out a wad of chewing tobacco, and crammed it into his mouth before answering. "He planned to be here when you were caught, but he bit off a little more than even a tough cuss like him could handle." Graven snickered. "It seems he ain't been on a horse since he was knee-high to a grasshopper. I guess they don't use them much in New York, or wherever the hell it is that he's from." He chewed a few seconds, his right cheek bulging. "All this hard riding has about done him in. When he walks, he looks like a duck trying to lay an egg."

Elizabeth Langtree finally spoke. "How dare you poke fun at him like that! The man is in pain, and all you can do is laugh at him behind his back?"

"Hell, lady. I'll do it to his face if it will make you happy," Graven said.

Fargo didn't know what to make of the exchange. For the schoolmarm to speak up for a man who might soon kill her was just plain ridiculous. Evidently she had yet to grasp the gravity of their predicament.

Hooves clattered on rock, and Benteen rode around the bend, leading another horse. Once Graven had climbed on, the two of them flanked Fargo.

"Keep this in mind, partner," the Texan said. "If you give us any fuss, that pretty little filly is going to wish you hadn't. Savvy?"

Fargo nodded. They had him over the proverbial barrel. He would not do anything to endanger Felicia. But that did not mean he wouldn't try something if the opportunity presented itself. As they rode out of the gully into the brilliant morning sunlight, he prayed to high heaven that it did.

12

The Texan turned out to be the gabby sort. He fancied the sound of his own voice as much as he did the rest of himself. When he wasn't talking, he would whistle or hum or sing bawdy saloon songs. They had been heading south for over two hours when he turned to Skye Fargo and remarked, "We found the breed, by the way. And you should have heard Morgan. I never met anyone who can cuss like him when he gets his dander up."

"Before I'm done, he'll do a lot more," Fargo vowed.

"Powerful words for a gent who won't be breathin' by this time tomorrow," Benteen said.

"Or sooner, if he gives us cause," Graven growled. "I owe this bastard, Tex. He nearly made wolf meat of me back in Denver."

Fargo held his peace. It would be unwise to provoke either of them. He needed the hired killers to relax their guard a little, just enough for him to slip a hand into one of his boots. Either that, or a distraction.

The three teachers would not be providing one. They trailed along silently, too wrapped up in their own thoughts to be of any use. Ernest Squib was leading the pack animals as Graven had directed him to do, his head bowed, oblivious to the world around him. Felicia was also distraught. Every now and then she would glare at her captors, but that was the extent of her defiance.

By contrast, Elizabeth Langtree did not appear upset at all. Thoughtful, yes, but she did not share the melancholy of her companions. Rather, she was as composed as if she were merely going for a Sunday jaunt in her hometown. She constantly scanned the rugged landscape before them, apparently seeking the first glimpse of the man responsible for placing them in peril.

Fargo didn't quite know what to make of her. He figured that she regarded the whole affair as an exciting lark. Like some others he had known, she was unable to come to grips with the fact that she might suffer and die. People like her reasoned that bad things always happened to others, never to them. They had to learn the hard way that life never played favorites.

Another half hour went by. Graven rode in front of Fargo, the cowboy behind him. The mountain man made it a point to shy away from thick brush and to swing around trees and bushes.

Then they rode over the crest of a hill. Below them lay a slope strewn with loose rocks and dirt. Footing for the horses would be treacherous, at best. Graven reined up to study the lay of the land, seeking another way down.

"What are you waitin' for?" Benteen asked.

"We should swing to the east about fifty or sixty yards," the mountain man said. "The slope there isn't as bad."

"Why waste the time?" the Texan said. "It's only twenty-five yards to the bottom. I can handle a hill like this in my sleep."

"You, maybe, but what about the greenhorns?" Graven said. "A raccoon could ride better than those three dunderheads combined. I don't want one of them taking a spill."

"So what if one does?" Benteen argued. "Morgan can't blame us if they bust a few bones because they can't ride worth a damn."

"I guess," Graven said, and began to descend, his sure-footed horse picking its way with delicate care, earth and stones clattering out from under it.

Fargo knew not to follow too closely. It was commonly understood that in such tricky situations riders should space themselves out. That way, if one went down, he didn't take others with him. But Fargo started down anyway. The sight of the slope had given him an idea, and to put it into effect he had to take a risk that might result in harm to his prized pinto as well as to himself.

Graven glanced around. "What the hell are you doing, jack-ass? Don't crowd me."

"I wasn't paying attention," Fargo lied. Contriving to turn the Ovaro so that its off side could not be seen by either the mountain man or the cowboy, he poked his left heel into the stallion's side, hard. The Ovaro started and took several quick strides.

"Damn it all! Didn't you hear me?" Graven bellowed.

"I'm trying to stop," Fargo said, while pretending to haul on the reins. At the same time he again jabbed with his heel. The stallion stumbled a few yards, causing bucketfuls of earth and rocks to come loose and slide down the hill, directly toward Graven's chestnut.

The mountain man swore when his mount shied away from the rattling talus. He had to grip his reins with both hands to maintain control.

Benteen found their antics amusing. "What a couple of id-iots!" he hooted. "Are Texans the only ones who know how to ride worth a damn?"

No one bothered to answer. Fargo was busy poking the Ovaro while slowly turning it sideways. The stallion, he knew was confused, and rightly so. He had never done anything like this before, never deliberately tried to make it slip and fall. A glance showed Graven having a hard time controlling the chestnut.

Fargo angled the Ovaro nearer. Neither of the killers guessed his intent. Graven was too busy trying to keep his mount up-right, and the arrogant cowboy was laughing his head off.

Fargo tensed for the next move in his calculated gambit. The Ovaro had slid to within a few feet of the chestnut, which would not calm down no matter what Graven did. The moun-tain man glared up at him, and Fargo chose that moment to rise in the stirrups and throw himself to the left while simulta-neously hauling on the reins with all his strength. It was more than enough to throw the Ovaro off balance. The next moment the stallion lost its footing and toppled over, crashing right into the chestnut.

Both horses whinnied wildly as they went down in a flurry of flying legs and tails. Fargo heard Felicia shout his name and the Texan snarl an oath as he threw himself from the saddle.

He made it look like an accident, made it seem like he was being thrown, when in reality he had launched himself at Graven. His shoulder caught the mountain man in the center of the chest and Graven left his saddle. Together they hit and tumbled down the slope.

When Fargo had launched himself from the Ovaro, he had slipped his right hand into the corresponding boot. When he slammed into Graven, he already had the Arkansas toothpick palmed. Now, in the act of tumbling, he grabbed the mountain man's shoulder and hung on tight.

"What the hell!" Graven roared as they were rolling on down the slope. "Let go of me, damn your hide!"

It had all happened so fast that no one knew Fargo had drawn his knife. If Graven had known it, he would never have twisted toward Fargo to shove him, giving Fargo the opening he needed. With a quick thrust, Fargo sank the slender blade between Graven's ribs, piercing the heart. The mountain man died with a look of astonishment lining his features.

Suddenly the two of them came to rest near the bottom of the hill. Fargo ended up on his left side, his left knee drawn up close to his chest so his boot was within easy reach. He feigned being knocked out and held himself perfectly still. Beside him lay Graven, belly down.

The clatter of more rocks told Fargo the Texan was on his way. Several rolling stones struck his back and legs. He did not so much as twitch. The fingers of his left hand rested inside the edge of his boot, less than an inch from the lawman's gift.

"Look at you clowns!" Benteen grumbled as he neared them. "A little fall like that, and you knock yourselves out. They sure do grow puny men in this part of the country."

The horse stopped. Fargo listened to a boot smack the ground, to the crunch of soles on gravel and the jingle of spurs as the Texan walked toward them. He had to be ready. If Benteen rolled Graven over first, he would have only a split second in which to react.

The Texan did indeed stop next to the mountain man. "Come on, pard. On your feet—"

Fargo rolled up onto his right knee, drawing the .32-caliber knuckle-duster as he did. Benteen had seen the knife jutting from Graven and his hand had swooped to his waist. The sun gleamed off a large derringer as it leaped clear of the cowboy's belt. Fargo beat him by a hair. The .32 cracked and a neat hole blossomed between Benteen's eyes. Somehow the Texan was still able to get off a shot, but the slug bit harmlessly into the dirt. Then Benteen crumpled, sprawling across Graven.

Gunsmoke curled upward from the knuckle-duster as Fargo checked to make certain both killers were no longer a threat. He reclaimed the toothpick, stuck both weapons back into his boots, and jerked the Colt from under Graven's belt. An inspection showed it had not been damaged.

Feeling like a whole man again, Fargo gathered their weapons and rose. The schoolteachers were lined up on the rim, too shocked by the violent turn of events to move or speak. He saw Graven's horse still on the ground, a foreleg bent at an unnatural angle, splintered bone poking through.

The Ovaro had not regained its feet, either. Dreading the worst, Fargo scrambled up the talus. Although scraped and cut, the pinto appeared otherwise unhurt. He made a thorough examination of all four legs before he hauled on the reins to get it to stand. Since they were closer to the bottom than the top, he led the Ovaro safely down.

Once the stallion was on level ground, Fargo shoved the pistol and derringer he had taken from the killers into a saddlebag, then drew his Colt and walked back up to the stricken chestnut. There was nothing he could do for the luckless animal. And since he couldn't bear the thought of it lying there for days on end, suffering a slow, agonizing death, he touched the barrel of the six-shooter to its head and fired once.

None of the teachers had a word to say at first after Fargo skirted the slope and rejoined them. He took the lead rope to the packhorses from Squib and trotted northward, taking it for granted they would follow.

Felicia drew alongside him. "Shouldn't we bury those men back there?"

"No," Fargo answered, surprised she would even suggest that they do.

"They were human beings, like us. They deserve proper burial, no matter what they did."

"They were vermin," Fargo amended. "And I wouldn't want to deprive the buzzards of a hearty meal."

"I had no idea you were such a hard man, Skye Fargo," Felicia said.

"It's a hard land," Fargo replied. He shifted to check on the others. Squib was closest, wearing a broad smile, mistakenly thinking the worst was behind him. Elizabeth Langtree had fallen much farther back than was usual for her and did not appear a smidgen as excited about their escape as she should be.

Fargo could hardly wait to question the pair, but for the time being he had to be patient. It was important that they put as many miles as they could behind them before sunset. Since the wind was blowing to the south, Morgan just might have heard the shots, even though he was miles off.

One fact gave Fargo a small measure of satisfaction. Having disposed of the mountain man, and having already taken care of the breed, he had eliminated the two best trackers in Frederick Morgan's employ. Unfortunately, between the mounts of his party and all their pack animals, they were leaving a trail a tenderfoot could follow. It wouldn't be hard for Morgan himself to track them.

Presently Fargo swung northwest of the route they had taken before. The country was rougher, the ground harder. It made for tougher going, but the ploy would also slow Morgan's band down a little. And every bit helped.

Later on Fargo changed course again, bearing due west. He had been through the area before and remembered something that might prove useful.

Until late evening Fargo forged deeper into the foothills. A stark peak reared to the northeast, a valley lay to the southwest. It was toward the former that Fargo bent their steps. By his reckoning they were several miles from the spot he wanted to reach when he had to stop in high timber. It was getting too dark to see, and the pack animals were exhausted.

"Why are we halting here?" Felicia said. "There is no water handy."

"We have no choice," Fargo said while dismounting. "One night without won't kill us." He let the reins drop, then took several steps to the right so he could see the other two ride up.

Squib took off his bowler and mopped his brow. "What a

day, eh?" he said, trying to act lighthearted. "I can't wait to turn in."

Elizabeth was fiddling with her saddlebags when she appeared, trying to close one but unable to because several folds of a green dress bulged out from under the flap. When she noticed Fargo, she faced front and straightened, her face impassive. "Why did you change direction?" she demanded.

"He did what?" Squib said anxiously.

"For the past few hours we've been heading west instead of north," Elizabeth said. "If you weren't so stupid, Ernest, you would have noticed long ago."

Fargo walked over to the schoolmaster's horse. "I want to know everything, and I want to know it now."

"Whatever are you talking about?" Squib responded. "Surely you didn't take those ruffians seriously? Until today, I never heard of that man they mentioned. What was his name—Morgan?"

"Liar," Fargo said, lunging. His fingers closed on the man's jacket, and with a quick wrench he heaved Squib overhead, then dashed him to the ground. Squib yelped when he hit, rolled, and tried to stand. Fargo was on him before he could. Bunching his fist, Fargo punched the teacher in the stomach.

"What are you doing?" Felicia cried. "Stop that this instant!"

Fargo paid no heed. He grabbed the front of Ernest Squib's shirt, snapped the man erect, and said coldly, "One more time. Tell me why Morgan is after you."

Even though he was in pain and quaking in fear like a hare caught in a steel trap, Squib replied, "Believe me when I say that I have no idea."

"Wrong answer," Fargo said pleasantly. He flicked his right fist twice, clipping the teacher on the chin. They were light blows, blows a frontiersman would have laughed at, but they were enough to send Squib staggering. The bowler fell from his limp fingers.

"Quit beating on him!" Felicia yelled while sliding to the ground. She ran up and grasped hold of Fargo. "You're behaving like the riffraff you killed. He could have you arrested."

Fargo motioned at the forest. "Are any of those trees wearing a badge?" Whipping around, Fargo backhanded Squib across the cheek and the schoolmaster tottered, then tripped over his own feet and landed on his posterior.

"No!" Felicia tried one more time. Darting between them, she extended her hands, palms outward. "Please, you must desist. What has he done to deserve such horrid treatment?"

"Thanks to him three innocent people were murdered," Fargo said, pushing her aside. Squib had risen to his knees and looked up in wide-eyed terror. Thinking of Melanie filled Fargo with rage. He lashed out, his foot catching Squib in the sternum.

The man landed on his back, then thrust out both arms and screeched like a piglet about to be slaughtered. "Don't hurt me any more!" he wailed. "I'll tell you everything! I swear!"

"I'm listening," Fargo said.

Squib slowly sat up and brushed dirt from his sleeve. He stared at the women as if expecting their support, but neither had a word to say. "It all started a few years ago when I lost my job at Arnhurst, a prestigious private school," he began. "There were allegations of improper conduct." Squib stopped and swallowed hard. "Anyhow, I found it difficult to obtain work. No other school cared to hire me. So, in desperation, I took to tutoring to make enough money to eat."

"Get to the point," Fargo prodded.

"Yes, well, it wasn't long before I was hired to tutor Frederick Morgan's twelve-year-old son in arithmetic and history. The boy had the attention span of a turnip, but I did the best I could."

Fargo made a threatening gesture.

"Hear me out! I want you to understand fully!" Squib declared. He inhaled a few times to steady himself. "I taught the boy at Morgan's house, a palatial estate fit for a king and queen. To give you some idea, there were gold chandeliers in several of the rooms. All the furniture, everything, was the finest money can by. I daresay that Morgan spent more on his china and silverware than I've made in my entire life to date."

"What did you steal?" Fargo asked, remembering the comments made by the Texan.

Squib gnawed on his lip a few seconds. "I'm getting to that," he said. "You see, I had been working there a while when it occurred to me that it might be possible to acquire a tidy nest egg that would last until I found regular work again."

"So you stole?" Elizabeth said, sounding appalled. "You violated Mr. Morgan's trust to line your own pockets?"

"It's not as simple as that," Squib said. "I'm trying to explain, but you're not listening. Morgan is a skinflint. He barely paid me enough for me to make ends meet. Yet he's so wealthy. I figured he wouldn't miss a few things."

"What kind of things?" Fargo asked.

"Oh, at first it was silverware. A few sterling silver forks fetched enough money to last me a week. So I began taking just about any small items I could smuggle out in my case. In six months' time I must have walked off with three thousand dollars worth of belongings." Squib paused. "And then I became greedy."

"Then?" Felicia said, making the single word a striking indictment.

Sweat beaded Squib's forehead and neck. He wiped his arm across his face before going on. "Morgan's wife was fond of jewelry. She owned priceless necklaces and bracelets and rings. I thought it would be easy to take something of hers, just one or two things that would be worth enough to set me up for years."

Fargo did not try to hide his disgust. "What did you take? A pearl necklace?"

"Nothing so simple," Squib said, and smiled, proud of himself. "I took a leather pouch containing ten of the biggest diamonds I had ever set eyes on."

"So that's what this is all about," Fargo said bitterly. "Morgan is trying to get the diamonds back."

The schoolmaster nodded. "I never thought it would come to this, believe me. I never expected anyone to die!" His voice tapered to a croak. "At the worst, I thought he would report the theft to the police and have me arrested. So I decided to leave before his wife noticed they were missing. That's why I answered the ad to teach on the frontier. I figured no one would ever find me out here."

The story cleared up a few puzzling points to Fargo's satisfaction, but not all of them. He realized that Morgan must have found out about Squib taking the job out West and traveled to

Denver to head the schoolmaster off. Maybe Morgan had known that three teachers were involved, and that one of them, Felicia, had been asking around town for a scout. Specifically, for him. And maybe Morgan had sent Dixie Lee to make sure he would not be in any shape to guide anyone anywhere.

So much, though was left unanswered. Why, Fargo wondered, did Morgan have Melanie and Erica and that other boarder slain, when none of them were connected in any way to Ernest Squib? Why hadn't Morgan simply corralled the thief in Denver instead of trailing him into the foothills? And finally, what about Edwards? Where had the desk clerk fit into the scheme of things? He posed that question to Squib.

"It was my doing. That day we arrived by stage, Felicia took us to the Imperial, where we had rooms reserved, and told us about the strange goings-on, about the man you chased. I guessed that Morgan was behind it. But I was not about to hand over his precious diamonds if I could help it. So long as he didn't find them on me, I could claim I was as innocent as a newborn baby."

"So you came up with a scheme," Fargo guessed.

Squib nodded. "That I did. I couldn't help but notice how Edwards felt about Felicia. He wore his feelings on his sleeve. After leaving the women, I looked him up and offered to buy him a drink. He confided in me after a few whiskeys. It was easy to convince him that she felt the same way, that all he had to do was follow us to the settlements and court her for a while, and before he knew it, they would be husband and wife."

"How could you?" Felicia said.

"What about the diamonds?" Fargo asked, to keep the man on track.

"Edwards didn't have enough money for all the supplies he needed, so I offered to buy some and told him that he could pay me back later. I hid the diamonds in the stuff I bought." Squib grinned. "That way, Morgan could have torn our whole camp apart and never found them."

Felicia jabbed a finger at him. "Didn't you realized the danger you were putting Mr. Edwards in?"

Elizabeth was standing a few feet off. She laughed and said, "He didn't care. All he's interested in are those gems."

"How dare—," Squib began, then puckered his brow and pointed to the southeast. "Say, is that who I think it is?"

Fargo turned. Less than two miles away, glittering brightly against the backdrop of inky woodland, sparkled a campfire.

13

It had been a trick. No sooner did Skye Fargo turn and set eyes on Morgan's campfire than Ernest Squib rose and bolted for the horses. Fargo wasn't caught napping, however. He pivoted, thrust out his left leg, and stood smiling while the schoolmaster smacked into the hard ground face first. Desperation inspired Squib to push to his hands and knees, and he was about to continue his mad dash when Fargo took a long stride and planted the tip of his boot in the thief's side.

Like a broken scarecrow, Squib crumpled and lay in the grass, sputtering and writhing.

Fargo flipped the teacher over and gripped the front of Squib's shirt. "Where are the diamonds?"

"I'll never—," Squib started to object, but got no further.

With a crisp pivot, Fargo slammed a fist into the man's abdomen. Squib cried out, then clutched himself in torment. "I can keep this up for as long as it takes," Fargo said, and shook the schoolmaster, as a terrier might shake a rat, to stress his point. "Spare yourself the pain. Tell me where the diamonds are hid."

"All right!" Squib screeched. "I'll show you! Just don't hurt me again."

Fargo heaved the man to his feet. Squib tottered as if drunk, steadied himself, and lurched over to the packhorses, to the animal that had belonged to Edwards. He fumbled at one of the ropes holding the supplies in place, managed to loosen it, and raised the canvas high enough to reveal a large leather pouch. This he removed.

"I had to be careful," Squib said as he placed the pouch on the ground and undid the leather knot that held the flap closed. "I didn't want Edwards to find the gems, so I had to put them in the last place he would ever look." From the pouch he drew a large jar of horehound candy and stroked it as a man might a lover.

"So you hid them in there?" Fargo said, not greatly impressed. "What if he had decided to help himself?"

"That was the genius of my plan," Squib said. "I've always had a sweet tooth, and when we stopped at the general store so I could indulge myself, Edwards mentioned that he hated the stuff. Couldn't stand the minty taste. Right then and there I knew what I had to do." Squib chuckled devilishly. "I asked him to bring this jar along. Told him that it would be hard to come by in the settlements and I wanted to have a supply on hand, but that I didn't want to take it with me for fear I'd eat the whole thing before we got there. And he believed me. The fool!"

Felicia Taugner surprised all of them by striding up to her peer and cuffing him across the mouth.

Squib rocked back on his heels, his hand over his lips. "What did you do that for?" he demanded, the words slurred.

"Because you are a truly despicable person," Felicia said, her tiny fists clenched to strike again. "Because you did unthinkable things to children. Because you stooped to robbery and then had the gall to try and justify your thievery. But most of all, because you use people as if they were your own personal puppets. You fill me with nothing but contempt, Ernest."

"Unless you've been in my shoes, you have no right to criticize," Squib said huffily.

"Save your story for the law," Fargo said, taking the jar from the schoolmaster's hands.

Squib made as if to grab it, but thought better of the idea. "What do you mean?" He scowled as Fargo began opening the container. "Are you going to turn me in?"

"For a teacher, you ask some mighty stupid questions," Fargo responded. "Or do you really think we'll let you ride off into the sunset as if nothing had happened?" He tossed the top aside and upended the jar, adding as the candy spilled out, "Yes, I'm turning you in. Just as soon as we see the ladies safely to the settlements, I'm taking you back to Denver and handing you over to Marshal Fedder. Then you'll be his headache."

The man's eyes glittered like those of a cornered rodent, but he prudently kept quiet.

Hunkering down, Fargo poked through the scattered horehound. He found a small pouch that had been stuffed into the center of the packed candy. Opening it over his palm, he let the contents trickle into his hand. The diamonds glittered dully in the dark, ten of them, each as big as his thumbnail.

"Goodness," Felicia said. "They're magnificent."

"That they are," Elizabeth agreed. "I can almost see how Ernest was tempted." She glanced at Fargo. "What will you do with them?"

"Turn the whole bunch over to Fedder," Fargo said. He fingered one of the stones, feeling its smooth finish, and wondered aloud how much all ten were worth.

"I don't know," Squib answered. "I never took them to a jeweler to have them appraised, for obvious reasons. My guess would be upwards of fifty thousand dollars."

"More like seventy-five," Elizabeth stated confidently.

Fargo replaced them, tied the pouch tight, and slid it into a pocket. He saw Squib's eyes linger and had no doubts the man would try to get them back, one way or another.

"An idea just struck me," Elizabeth declared, "a way we can put an end to this nightmare and come out of it alive." She pointed at the distant fire. "If all Morgan cares about are those diamonds, I say we should hand them over so he'll go away and leave us alone. In fact, I'm willing to be the one who rides over to deliver the pouch. What do you say?"

"I say it is too risky," Felicia said.

"But if I'm willing to take the chance, what harm can it do?" Elizabeth countered. "Just think. We can go on about our business without having to look over our shoulders every minute of every day."

"And what if Morgan decides to do the same to you that he did to those poor women in Denver?" Felicia asked. "You might wind up horribly butchered."

"I'm willing to take the gamble," Elizabeth insisted, and held out her right hand to Fargo. "What do you say, big man? Fork them over."

"No."

The corners of Elizabeth's mouth crimped. "Why not? Are you sure you're not planning on keeping them yourself?"

Fargo merely looked at her until she averted her gaze. Stepping to the Ovaro, he gripped the saddle horn and swung up. "There's another way to end this once and for all. I want the three of you to stay put until I return. Don't make a fire. Eat jerky if you're hungry."

"What are you going to do?" Felicia inquired.

"What has to be done," was all Fargo would say. He slipped his fingers into his left boot and pulled out the knuckle-duster. "Do you know how to use this?"

"Me?" Felicia blinked. "You must be joking. My parents frowned on firearms. I've never once fired a gun, my whole life long."

"I have," Elizabeth volunteered, once again offering her hand. "Just tell me what you have in mind."

Fargo balked at turning the pistol over to the beauty. He would much rather have given it to Felicia, but it was plain the very idea scared her. Yet they needed a gun to protect themselves. "Here," he said, setting it in Elizabeth's palm. "Just in case. If Squib tries to ride off, shoot him in the leg. If he tries to hurt either of you, shoot him in the chest. And if he tries to come after me, empty the gun in his head."

"You can rely on me," Elizabeth said, hefting the .32.

Nodding, Fargo gave Felicia a reassuring glance, then wheeled the pinto and headed to the southeast. He hoped to catch Morgan's bunch napping. There were only three killers left: Pony Deal, the gambler; Dixie Lee, his pard; and the black man, the one with the build of a blacksmith. With a little luck, he might be able to dispose of all of them before they got off more than two or three shots.

Once Fargo judged he was within five hundred yards of their camp, he drew rein and advanced on foot. Although he disliked leaving the Sharps behind, he did so. When up against superior odds, speed was crucial. And he could fire the Colt five times in the same amount of time it would take him to fire the big rifle twice.

Fargo stalked silently forward, gliding like a spectral ghost from cover to cover. He counted two figures seated within a few feet of the fire, blankets draped over their shoulders. Two others had already turned in. It gave him pause, until he realized they had probably turned in early to get the jump on his party the next day. Well, they were in for a nasty shock.

Seventy-five yards out, Fargo sank onto his belly. Snaking through high grass and around an occasional mesquite, he came within pistol range. The two men by the fire were talking in low tones. Firelight reflected off the sinister features of Pony Deal and Frederick Morgan.

The former was the most deadly. A gunman of Deal's caliber would be lightning fast and deadly accurate. Which earned Deal the distinction of being the first one Fargo would shoot.

Soon Fargo was close enough to eavesdrop. He froze when Deal abruptly stood, but the gambler was only interested in pouring another cup of coffee for Morgan and himself.

"I'll be glad when this mess is behind us," Deal was saying. "For some time I've been thinkin' of headin' on down to New Orleans. The climate there is a hell of a lot warmer than in Denver, and a man can make a good livin' at cards."

"Provided he wins often enough," Morgan noted.

Deal smirked. "I win nine times out of ten. It's all in how the cards are shuffled and dealt."

"I trust you're not admitting you cheat?" Morgan said good-naturedly. "It was my understanding that professionals in your class rarely resort to trickery."

"Don't believe everything you hear," Pony Deal said. "When a man's livelihood depends on the luck of the draw, you can bet your bottom dollar he'll do whatever it takes to make sure the draw works in his favor." The gambler lifted his tin cup.

Frederick Morgan leaned back. "We have more in common than I would have suspected. A businessman like myself must also stack the deck if he is to turn a tidy profit."

Deal imitated the other's tone when he replied, "I trust you're not admittin' that you cheat your customers?"

"Nothing like that," Morgan said. "There are other ways of insuring that one comes out ahead. Long ago I learned to vary my interests, to dip each hand into a different pie, if you will." His expression hardened. "Everything was going along smoothly until that runt of a bookworm, Squib, became too damn greedy for his own good."

"Do you still think he had the whole thing planned from the moment he started teachin' your son?" Deal asked.

"I don't know," Morgan said thoughtfully. "At first I assumed all three were in cahoots, since they were all heading west together. But I might have been wrong." He took a sip of coffee. "Not that it matters. They have to die anyway."

"Just say the word, mister," Deal said. "You're the one forkin' over all the money. Whoever you want out of the way is as good as dead."

Fargo had been edging forward the whole time and was now within eight feet of the pair. The men on the ground had not so much as budged. Tucking his legs up under him, he suddenly sprang upright and covered all four. To his surprise, neither Morgan nor the gambler made an outcry or tried to unlimber a weapon. They both merely stared at him, as calm as if they were attending a church social.

"You won't be killing anyone else, Morgan," Fargo announced. "It stops here."

"Do tell," Morgan said, unruffled.

The gambler had the look of a cat that had just swallowed a canary. "So we meet again, mister. I don't mind tellin' you that you've made us earn our keep. I never thought anyone would get the better of Graven, let alone the breed."

"You should have stayed back East," Fargo told Morgan as he warily moved closer. "You would have spared yourself a lot of trouble."

"And miss out on all this wonderful scenery?" Morgan said. "If nothing else, I should thank Squib for showing me where I should bring my wife for our next vacation."

"She'll be taking it by herself," Fargo said, halting. He glanced at the sleepers, who had yet to awaken. "There's one thing I want to know before we end it, Morgan. Why did you have those people in Denver killed? They knew nothing about Squib, nothing about the theft."

"They knew you," Morgan said.

"But I had no idea what you were up to," Fargo said. "Squib didn't tell me about stealing your diamonds until just a short while ago."

"I had no way of knowing," Morgan stated. "But it wouldn't have made a difference. I have to bury everyone connected with this in any way whatsoever. The schoolmarms. Those people in Denver. I can't leave a single one alive."

"Why the hell not?" Fargo asked, about convinced the man killed for the sheer sake of killing.

"Because of a fact of which you are unaware," Morgan said suavely. "Something not even Squib knows." He peered into the night as if seeking the cause of all his woes. "Those diamonds, Trailsman, were not mine to begin with."

"What?" Fargo said.

"Some of my vast business interests are less than legitimate," Morgan said, smiling. "I stole those stones from a rich Arab who has been searching for them ever since. He suspects me, but has no proof." The smile faded. "I simply can't afford to have the slightest mention of them spread around. There's no telling who might hear."

The full implication hit Fargo like a physical blow. "Are you saying that you had all those people killed on the off chance they might have heard something?"

Morgan nodded, showing no remorse at all. "And I'm not done yet. After you are disposed of, I'll attend to the teachers."

"You're forgetting one thing," Fargo said, leveling the Colt. "This."

"Oh?" Frederick Morgan set down his cup. "Do you have what it takes to shoot a man in cold blood? Can you squeeze the trigger when the man facing you is unarmed?" So saying, he slowly pulled his coat wide open to show he did not have a gun strapped on.

Fargo took one last step. "After what you've done, mister, I could shoot you if you had your back turned to me."

"My compliments, then. Few men have the inner fortitude to do as you would. Few men nowadays have the raw courage we do."

"How can you call yourself brave?" Fargo said, inclined to laugh, "when you hire others to do all your killing for you?"

"Not all," Morgan said. "On occasion I like to give those who have proven to be a source of annoyance my personal touch." A wicked grin lit his face. "Take that whore, for instance. What was her name again? Marsha?"

"Melanie," Fargo said, fury building within.

"Whatever. She was hardly worth the bother, but I carved her up myself. After I strangled her with my bare hands, of course." Morgan held his hands out and turned them over a few times, admiring them. "The hussy put up a terrific fight. You should have been there."

"Bastard!" Fargo practically shouted, on the verge of flying into a rage. Too late, he realized that the two sleeping killers should have awakened by this time. Too late, he glanced closely at them and discovered they were not sleeping figures at all but blankets spread out over saddles. Far too late, Fargo sensed there was someone behind him. He tried to turn.

It seemed as if a falling tree crashed down onto Fargo's back. He barely flung his hands in front of him in time to absorb the jolt of impact with the ground. Iron fingers grabbed his right wrist to keep him from using the Colt. Other hands seized his other wrist. A foot smashed into his kidney, and his body went weak all over of its own accord. He was savagely jerked straight up. The Colt was torn from his grasp.

Through a spinning haze, Fargo saw the black man on one side, Dixie Lee on the other, both beaming over how cleverly they had duped him.

Frederick Morgan slowly stood and took a step. "So much for your bluster, Mr. Fargo. Didn't it occur to you that this whole setup might be a trap? That I had these men deliberately build the fire up nice and big so you would be sure to spot it? That I was luring you in to spare myself the time and effort of hunting you down?"

Fargo was too ashamed of himself to say a word. He had fallen for one of the oldest tricks around, and all because he had been too eager to put an end to the ordeal. He had let his craving for vengeance cloud his judgment.

"There's no need to speak," Morgan rubbed it in. "Your face gives you away. If it's any consolation, Mr. Deal was correct. You have proven most bothersome." He held out a hand to the black man. "If you would be so kind, Mr. Latham. His pistol, please."

Fargo found himself staring down the barrel of his own revolver. He struggled to regain control of his limbs.

Pony Deal had risen but did not come around the fire. He

acted bored by the whole affair and had not even bothered to put down his tin cup. "Get this over with, will you?" he remarked. "In the morning we'll go find the teachers, and by tomorrow night we'll be well on our way to Denver."

"Be patient," Morgan said. "Or, as they say out here, hold your horses, Mr. Deal. After all the time and money this has cost me, I feel that I'm entitled to have a little fun." He looked at Dixie. "Mr. Lee, do you have that folding knife of yours?"

"Sure do, boss."

"Give it to me. Fargo, here, was so moved by my treatment of that whore, I feel it is only fair to do the same to him."

Dixie Lee cackled. "Do you aim to strangle him afterward? That would be a sight to see. I've never seen a man choked to death before."

"What an excellent idea," Morgan said.

The short killer in the heavy coat had to take one hand off of Fargo's wrist to reach for the folding knife. It was the moment Fargo needed, the only one he was likely to get. As Dixie Lee let him go, he tore his left arm loose, grabbed Dixie's coat, and shoved him into Morgan. The mastermind was caught flat-footed, and the two of them staggered backward into the fire. Dixie Lee yelped and leaped clear, straight into Pony Deal, who was going for his six-shooter.

All this Fargo glimpsed as he swung toward the huge black. man Latham cocked a fist to smash him in the face. Fargo ducked under the blow, then drove his right boot into Latham's knee. There was a loud crack. Latham grimaced and swayed, his grip on Fargo's wrist slackening enough for Fargo to tear free.

"Kill him!" Morgan roared.

Fargo did not delay an instant. Whirling, he sped into the darkness as behind him pistols cracked in thundering cadence. Slugs whizzed through the air or bit into the earth all around him. How the killers missed, he would never know. But in seconds he was in the clear and weaving madly as he sped deeper into the gloom.

"After him, damn you! Don't let the son of a bitch get away!"

Morgan sounded ready to burst a blood vessel. It was Fargo's only consolation as he thought of the blunder he had made and the price he had almost paid. A glance revealed Pony Deal, Dixie Lee and Latham in pursuit, the huge man limping badly. They had fanned out and were zigzagging to cover more ground as they ran. All three had revolvers. All Fargo had was the Arkansas toothpick.

Hunching over, Fargo drew up short behind some sage. The Ovaro, he reckoned, should be northwest of his position. In order to prevent the killers from stumbling on it, he must divert them in the opposite direction.

Dipping lower, Fargo felt along the ground until he found a stone. He snapped his arm back and threw as far as he could to the southeast. The stone was a blur soon lost in the night. He heard it hit, though, and so did the killers. Dixie Lee and Pony Deal both fired. In concert, they closed on the spot.

At last something had gone right. Fargo made for the stallion, staying low. He saw Frederick Morgan by the fire, easy pickings for a man with a rifle. Fargo couldn't wait to get his hands on the Sharps.

A few strides later, Fargo halted as if he had smashed into an invisible wall. It had dawned on him that Latham had disappeared. He scoured his vicinity, leery of making another mistake. Considering how hard he had kicked Latham's knee, it was possible the man had been unable to bear his own weight and had collapsed. Then again, Latham was built like a redwood. Nothing short of death would slow a man like him down.

Drawing the toothpick, Fargo cautiously went on. The five hundred yards seemed more like a thousand. He longed to see the Ovaro, and in due course spied its outline up ahead. Pony Deal and Dixie Lee were nowhere near, and Morgan was still bathed in the glow from the fire.

Twenty feet from the pinto, Fargo paused. He debated whether to try a rifle shot from that range. If he could pick off Morgan, the rest might scatter. He had turned to go the rest of the way when to his fleeting astonishment a part of the earth itself seemed to rear up and embrace him in a constricting hug.

Only it wasn't the earth.

It was Latham. And he had Fargo in a bear hug that could crush the life from a real bear.

14

Skye Fargo had fought some strong men in his wide-flung travels. Rough-and-tumble lumberjacks, rowdy river men, hardy ranchers, saloon brawlers, Indian warriors—he had gone up against all kinds at one time or another. But never had he faced an enemy as enormously strong as Latham. Being caught in the huge man's massive arms was like being pinned between two gigantic slabs of rock.

Fargo strained and heaved with all his might, yet it did no good. He tried to butt Latham in the face with his forehead, but the man jerked aside. He tried to knee Latham in the groin, but no matter where he hit, it was like hitting stone.

Latham wore a taunting grin. "You hurt me, mister," he growled. "Hurt me bad. So now I repay the favor."

The reminder was timely. Fargo arched both legs back as far as he could, then drove his knees into Latham's. The bigger man flinched and sagged but refused to go down. Fargo did it again, with more force. The shattered knee buckled and they fell to one side.

Latham shifted, trying to land on top of Fargo, where he could use his greater weight to maximum advantage.

Wrenching to the right before they hit the ground, Fargo succeeded in flipping them partially over. His right shoulder took most of the impact. For a few heartbeats Latham's face was inches from his own. In a flash he rammed his brow into the killer's nose, while at the selfsame moment he slammed his knee up between Latham's legs.

At last the brawny arms encircling Fargo relaxed. Not much, but enough for him to exert himself and break free. He scrambled to get out of reach, and Latham came after him, grabbing for his neck. Fargo swatted Latham's hand aside, rose to one knee, and slid the toothpick from its sheath.

"You're a dead man!" Latham declared, lunging.

Pivoting on one heel, Fargo speared the narrow blade into his attacker's chest. He tried for a killing stroke, but at the very last instant Latham shifted just enough to spare his heart. A cuff to the head knocked Fargo down again. Latham, in agony, began to retreat, a hand over the wound.

Fargo scooped loose dirt into his left hand as he rose. He feinted with the bloody toothpick. Latham naturally focused on the knife and never saw the flick of Fargo's other wrist that resulted in dirt flying into Latham's eyes. The bigger man's automatic reaction was to bring both hands up to his face.

Diving forward, Fargo buried the Arkansas toothpick a second time. He avoided a punch that would have cracked his skull, then swiftly stabbed his foe several times. Before Latham could retaliate, he leaped to the left.

Latham sagged like a punctured balloon, his hands the only thing that kept him from pitching onto his stomach. Lifting his head, he actually grinned. "You're damn good, mister. The best," he said weakly.

Fargo held himself ready in case it was a ruse.

"I hope you kill that bastard, Morgan," Latham went on. "Never did like him. If only he didn't pay so damn well." Latham's face contorted. "Sorry about your woman. I don't cotton to murdering females."

"Morgan will get his," Fargo vowed.

Latham nodded once, groaned, and collapsed.

Quickly Fargo took the dead man's pistol, a Colt similar to his own, and shoved it in his holster. As he moved toward the Ovaro, gunfire crackled. Pony Deal and Dixie Lee were charging toward him with their pistols blazing. Fargo replied once and saw them dive for cover.

The Ovaro had its head high and was poised for flight. As Fargo vaulted into the saddle, the pinto broke into a gallop. More shots punctuated their flight, but none scored.

Fargo rode for several minutes, then reined up and looked over his shoulder. The fire had been extinguished. If he tried to sneak on back, they would be waiting for him. He'd sneak right into an ambush.

Disappointed that he had blown his chance to end it, Fargo rode on. He had a backup plan that might work, provided he could persuade one of the teachers to lend a hand. When, much later, their clustered horses appeared, he slowed and called out, "Don't shoot. I'm coming in." It paid to be extra careful where greenhorns were concerned.

A figure emerged from the pines and stood awaiting him. Fargo saw that it was Elizabeth Langtree, holding the knuckle-duster. "Where are the others?" he asked as he stepped down.

"We thought it best to hide," Elizabeth said, bobbing her chin at the trees. "What about you? Are Morgan and his men dead?"

"One is," Fargo said. "A man named Latham." He walked a few yards to the east and attuned his ears to the sounds of the night, trying to determine if the killers had followed him. She dogged his steps.

"It seems to me that you're going to an awful lot of trouble to pay back a man who isn't worth losing your life over."

"I'm not doing this for him," Fargo said, wishing she would be quiet so he could listen. "I'm doing it because of those three people Morgan killed."

"Four," Elizabeth said.

"There was another one I don't know about?" Fargo asked absently while surveying the terrain.

"Yes," Elizabeth said.

"Who?"

"A schoolmarm who refused to cooperate with Morgan when he asked her to be his spy and keep her eyes on Taugner and Squib. Her name was Elizabeth Langtree."

Fargo stiffened. Suddenly her behavior made all the sense in the world. He went to turn, starting his draw as he did, but froze when the knuckle-duster was jammed into the base of his spine.

"I wouldn't, handsome, if I were you," the woman said, and took the Colt. "Behave and you'll live a while longer." She stepped back several paces. "I should blow a hole in you after all the headaches you've caused us, but knowing dear Frederick as I do, I imagine he'll want the honor of disposing of you himself." The hammer of the Colt clicked. "You can turn around if you want."

Hands out from his sides, Fargo slowly faced her. "So you've been working for him all along?"

The woman nodded. "For years, in fact. It's safe to say I see more of the man than his wife does." She chuckled. "In more ways than one."

"How—," Fargo began.

"How did I switch places with the real Langtree?" she interrupted. "It was easy as pie. Once Morgan discovered the theft, he hired a policeman who was on the take to do some checking. The cop intercepted some of Squib's mail and later replaced it. That's how Morgan learned about the teaching positions. He was able to track down the real Langtree before she left to join the others." She shook her head at the memory. "What a stupid bitch. Morgan explained everything to her and offered her money to keep tabs on the others, but she refused. Told him she was going to the law. He couldn't allow that." The wind fanned her hair. "It also made him suspicious that all three were in it together somehow. I tell you, that man doesn't trust a living soul. Not even his own mother."

"Why didn't you show your hand sooner?" Fargo wondered.

"I was under orders not to. Morgan wanted me as his ace in the hole. I was only to act if I was sure of getting my hands on the diamonds and returning them to him." She grinned. "Fork them over, big man."

"Do you have a name?" Fargo asked as he slipped a hand into his pocket.

"Jessica Tandy, at your service." She gave a little mock bow but did not take her eyes off him. "Don't get any ideas. Just because I'm a woman doesn't mean I can't pull the trigger. I've done it before."

"You're just another hired killer," Fargo said in scorn to provoke her. "No better than Charley Crow or Graven." He let the small pouch dangle from his index finger by the leather loop that served as the tie, then twirled it faster and faster.

Tandy laughed. "I'm not childish enough to fall for such a blatant trick. Give them to me—now."

"Whatever you want," Fargo said. He deliberately let the loop slip off and the pouch sailed clear over her head. Tandy did what anyone else would have done—she never took her gaze off the pouch. As she leaned her head back, Fargo sprang, grasping both of her wrists and shoving her arms wide to keep her from shooting him. The knuckle-duster went off, the slug going wild. Fargo tried to shove her to the ground but found he had a wildcat on his hands.

The woman hurled herself backward in an attempt to break his grip. She kicked at his shins, at his knees. She tried to drive her own knee into his manhood.

Twisting and shifting, Fargo evaded most of her blows. One landed on his right shin and he thought his leg would give out. He forked a foot behind her and pushed in an effort to trip her, but she jumped over his foot, then bent, her mouth wide, her teeth about to tear into his wrist. To ward her off, Fargo swung her to the right, throwing her off stride, and then, releasing her right wrist, he punched her squarely on the jaw.

Jessica Tandy melted to the grass, the Colt and the knuckle-duster falling beside her.

Fargo picked up both guns, found the diamonds, and hastened into the trees. If Tandy was half as bloodthirsty as her lover, Felicia must be dead, he feared. He had gone only a few yards when he nearly tripped over someone lying facedown.

Squatting, Fargo discovered it was Ernest Squib, not the schoolmarm. A dark stain on the thief's shirt showed the cause of death. From the look of things, Tandy had shoved the knuckle-duster against his side and fired twice.

But what about Felicia? Fargo asked himself as he rose. Making a complete turn, he sought some sign of her. There was none. He went twenty feet to the west, then made a wide circuit of the area, checking behind trees and in high weeds. She was nowhere to be found.

Suddenly the breeze brought the sound of a groan. Fargo made a beeline for the source of the sound, and came on Felicia in the act of sitting up and rubbing her head. "How badly are you hurt?" he asked, sinking down next to her.

"Skye? Thank goodness." Felicia sagged against him. "For some reason, Elizabeth hit me. She led me into these trees under the pretext of wanting to have a few words with me alone, and as soon as I turned my back on her, she knocked me out." Felicia gazed in all directions. "Where is she? Why would she do such a thing?"

Fargo explained briefly while helping her to stand. "We

have to get out of here," he concluded. "Morgan and his men might be closing in on us."

"Poor Ernest," Felicia said on seeing the corpse. "He should have left well enough alone. Tutoring would not have made him rich, but at least he would have made ends meet. And it beats being dead."

The horses were all where they should be, but Jessica Tandy was not. Fargo took the fact in stride. He had a hunch she had revived, heard them coming, and dashed off so quickly she had neglected to take a mount. Well, he wasn't about to leave her one. "We have to put a few miles behind us by morning," he announced, guiding the schoolmarm to her animal.

"Why not make a stand right here?" Felicia suggested. "We can't hope to outrun them with all the horses we have."

"We'll make a stand soon enough," Fargo informed her, "but I have a better place in mind." After boosting her into the saddle, he forked leather and walked the Ovaro to the northwest, relying upon the stars to point the way.

"I hope you know what you're doing," Felicia said. "I don't care to end up like Mr. Squib."

Fargo hoped so, too. Riding at night through a thick forest was a hazardous proposition. He made her ride close to him so he could alert her to obstacles. The pack animals were making a lot of noise, which he minded, but they were also leaving a trail Morgan would have no problem following, which suited him just fine. He wanted the butcher to come after them.

It was not much shy of midnight when Fargo drew rein at the mouth of a gorge. "We'll camp here," he said.

"I'm glad," Felicia responded. "I'm so tired and sore I can barely stay awake." She slipped dismounting and would have fallen had she not snatched at the saddle horn for support.

"Are you hungry?" Fargo asked while stripping off his bedroll.

"Not really, not after everything that has happened today. I'm beginning to think taking this job was the worst decision of my life." Felicia took her own bedroll and moved to a flat, clear spot. "You tend to the horses and I'll arrange everything."

"Fair enough." Fargo tossed his bedroll to her, then tethered the stock. It took a while, and when he was done, he was surprised to see that the schoolmarm had made a single bed wide enough for two people. He sat down and looked at her pretty face, peeking at him over the edge of the blanket. "I thought you claimed you were tired."

"I am," Felicia said. "I'm also cold. Crawl in here and warm me up."

Fargo doubted her motive, but he did as she wanted. There was no harm in indulging, as far as he could tell. They had a substantial lead on Morgan, which made it highly unlikely the band of killers would show up until several hours after sunrise. Removing his spurs and gun belt, he placed them within easy reach, lifted the blanket, and crawled in.

"Isn't this cozy, Skye?" Felicia asked, snuggling against him. "I'm warmer already."

Only then did Fargo learn she was naked. She nestled her head on his shoulder, molding herself to him. His hand touched her smooth back and he traced the length of her spine with a finger. She quivered, then pecked him on the neck.

"I like that."

"You're loco," Fargo said, and rolled onto his side so they were nose to nose. Even if he had wanted to abstain, which he did not, the stirring in his loins would have been enough to change his mind. He planted his lips on hers and was delighted by the hunger she displayed. One of her hands tugged at his shirt, slipped underneath, and roved over his chest, while the other loosened his pants and delved below his hips. He was rock hard in the bat of an eye.

"It's nice to see you still want me," Felicia commented. "I didn't know if you would be in the mood."

"A man is always in the mood," Fargo said, and smothered her mouth with more kisses. Her pliant, warm body wriggled deliciously. His hand massaged her backside, eliciting a gasp of raw pleasure.

Fargo's weariness had evaporated, and hers, evidently, as well. He kneaded a breast until she cooed like a lovebird, then replaced his palm with his mouth. Felicia removed his hat so she could play with his hair. Her nails dug into him when he tweaked both of her hard nipples at the same time.

"You sure know how to help a gal relax."

Grinning, Fargo rubbed her inner thighs. She parted her legs to receive him but he was not ready yet. Sliding his hands under her arms, he scooted her higher, stopping when her twin globes were suspended in front of his face. She shivered when he licked first one nipple, then the other. Her hand lightly rubbed his pole, cupped his jewels.

Fargo eased onto his back and positioned her on top of him. He slid his right hand between her legs and brushed his finger across her womanhood, which caused her to mew and arch her spine like a she-cat in heat. When he inserted a finger into her inner sheath, she held herself still for a few moments. then ground into his hand with passionate abandon. His knuckles pressed on her pleasure knob, inciting her lust further.

The cool breeze played over their bodies. Fargo hiked down his pants, exposing himself. Felicia fondled him, her mouth curled in a hungry grin, and ran a palm up across his stomach and chest.

"You're magnificent," she said huskily, "like a thorough-bred stallion."

Fargo kissed her, burying his tongue in her mouth. She sucked on it, her cheeks working in and out, her bottom continuing to grind into his balled hand. Soon his fingers were slick with her juices.

"I want you more than words can ever say," Felicia said.

"Then don't talk," Fargo advised, attaching his lips to an earlobe. From there he licked a path down across her neck to her breasts, which were swollen with desire. He squeezed both and she humped her bottom. Her eyes were closed, her features more relaxed than they had been all day.

Fargo could feel the tension draining out of him, too. Wrapping his hands around her narrow hips, he lifted her into the air, then guided her down at an angle until she was impaled on his manhood. Felicia licked her rosy lips in anticipation. She began rocking on her knees to move her hips in a steady pumping rhythm.

Neither of them were in any rush. Fargo let her enjoy herself. His hands dallied at her breasts and roamed her silken skin. For her part, she dug her nails into his shoulders and every so often leaned down to kiss him.

Somewhere close at hand a wolf wailed, but neither of them paid any attention. Fargo knew that wolves seldom attacked humans, and Felicia was so lost in her personal rapture that she would not have cared if a grizzly were to rear out of the night. For the longest while the slap of their bodies was like a muted drumbeat.

Felicia was the first to reach the brink. She stiffened, cried out in a throaty purr, then drove into him in a frenzy of unbridled lust. When she reached the pinnacle, she called his name softly, over and over.

Fargo was about ready. He firmed his grip on her hips for leverage and pumped into her with increasing speed and force. The faster he went, the more ecstasy he felt. When the explosion came, as it inevitably did, he thought he would shear her in half from the urgency of his thrusts.

"Oh! Oh! Oh!" Felicia panted. "Don't ever stop! Never!"

She was asking the impossible. Fargo had more stamina than most, but at length he had drained himself dry and had no recourse but to coast to a weary stop. She collapsed on top of him, her nipples gouging into his chest.

"Thank you, Skye."

"Any time."

Fargo groped beside them until he located the Colt. With the pistol in one hand and his other resting on the schoolmarm's back, he fell asleep. This time he slept lightly, awakening at the slightest of sounds. Once the snap of a twig brought him around and he sat up and leveled the six-shooter. Shortly thereafter a raccoon wandered up. It stood on its hind legs and sniffed a few times, then waddled off. Fargo lay back down after covering the two of them to ward off the chill night wind.

Dawn was an hour away when Fargo roused himself and swiftly dressed. He let Felicia catch extra winks while he hiked a few hundred feet to a barren knob that afforded a sweeping view of the countryside they had covered the night before. As yet, no dust showed, but it was just a matter of time. Morgan would be eager to finish it.

Felicia was fully dressed and seated cross-legged when he returned. "You had me worried. I didn't know where you had gotten to."

"Just checking," Fargo said. "I'll get a fire going if you'll fix the coffee."

154

"Should we?" Felicia asked in surprise. "I mean, with them after us and all? Won't the smoke give us away?"

"I want them to see it," Fargo said, but did not elaborate. He soon had flames crackling loudly and went about loading the pack animals and saddling the mounts while she made a fresh pot of coffee.

It was plain as the nose on her face that Felicia was uneasy, and growing more so as the minutes ticked by. She took the cup he gave her but hardly touched it. Repeatedly she glanced to the southeast. Finally she could take the suspense no longer and declared, "I think we're making a mistake. We should go on before they get here."

"In due time," Fargo said.

"You have a plan, don't you? Why won't you confide in me?"

Fargo saw no reason not to. "Did you ever try to catch birds when you were a kid?"

Felicia shook her head. "Can't say as I ever did. Behavior like that was frowned on. Proper young ladies do not go around trapping animals."

"I remember one summer when a bunch of us were catching every bird within fifty miles," Fargo reflected. "We got our hands on an old crate and rigged it with a branch and twine so that when a bird went under the crate to eat the seed we'd spread around, we'd pull on the twine and the box would come crashing down."

"Oh, I've seen children do that before," Felicia said.

"We're about to do the same," Fargo revealed. Nodding at the gorge, he said, "There's our crate. The seed will be our horses. You'll be the twig. And I'll be the twine."

"I'm still not sure I follow."

"You will," Fargo told her, and swallowed more coffee. He was on his third cup when four riders appeared, crossing a far-off clearing, no more than stick figures at that distance. "Company is coming to call," he said dryly.

"Now do we do something?" Felicia asked hopefully.

"That we do." Fargo drained the last of his coffee and placed the cup in one of his saddlebags. He kicked enough dirt on the fire to produce clouds of smoke, but not enough to extinguish it entirely. Then he took Felicia's hand and steered her to her horse. "Mount up."

Once the schoolmarm had obeyed, Fargo pointed to a bend in the gorge, not quite a hundred yards off. "I want you to ride to that first bend and stop. Don't go around it until you are sure Morgan has seen you. Then ride like hell. And don't come back unless you hear me holler."

"Where will you be?"

Fargo walked to the Ovaro and yanked the Sharps from the boot. He indicated an immense boulder to the right of the gorge. "I'll be back there, waiting to jerk on the twine."

Felicia did not like the plan and it showed. "I don't want to leave you," she objected. "Can't we stick together?"

"No," Fargo said bluntly. Placing a hand on her leg, he looked into her eyes. "If there was a better way, I'd do it. All I ask is that you promise to light a shuck to Denver if something happens to me. Head south. In a few days you'll be there. Marshal Fedder will protect you."

Reluctantly Felicia agreed, adding, "I hate this. I don't want anything to happen to you."

"Makes two of us," Fargo said. "Now be on your way. It will probably be an hour or so before they show up."

"Then why not wait a while yet?"

"They might have a spyglass," Fargo said, alluding to the practice started by the old-time mountain men of toting a small telescope along when out in the wild. Many a white man had saved his own scalp by spotting hostiles long before the hostiles spied him.

Stepping back, Fargo gave her horse a light smack on the rump, and it headed into the gorge. The other animals trailed along, strung in a line, making plenty of fine tracks in dirt that had not been touched by a hoof since Fargo last went through the area over a year before.

Fargo waited until she had reined up short of the bend, then he waved and went behind the boulder. Leaving the Ovaro in its shadow, he moved to the edge, cocked the Sharps, and leaned his shoulder on the smooth surface.

The sun slowly arced into the blue vault above. In the trees a flock of sparrows frolicked, until all of a sudden they took wing with much agitated chirping. Fargo knew the moment of truth was almost upon him.

Dixie Lee was the first to appear, riding out from the pines with the stock of a rifle propped on his leg. His floppy hat had been pushed back on his head, and for once he was not wearing the heavy coat. He scanned the area leading up to the mouth of the gorge, focusing on the fire.

Fargo saw the killer say something over a shoulder. Moments later Pony Deal joined his partner and they advanced together. Behind them, Frederick Morgan and Jessica Tandy warily rode into the open.

Dixie Lee was studying the ground, reading tracks. At the fire, he swung down and kicked the smoking embers. "They left just a short while ago," he announced.

"Hell," Pony Deal said. "Any idiot could tell that."

Dixie jabbed a finger at the gunman gambler. "What are you picking on me for? It wasn't my fault Fargo got away last night."

"You were the one he heaved like a feather," Pony Deal said. "If you hadn't knocked Morgan into me, I would have shot Fargo dead then and there and we'd be well on our way back by now."

Frederick Morgan halted behind the gambler. "Enough of this damned bickering! I hired you to dispose of those who annoy me, not drive me crazy with your childish antics."

Behind the boulder, Fargo wedged the Sharps to his shoulder. He was careful not to poke the barrel into the sunlight. Aligning the sights, he took a steady bead on Deal. As much as he would rather shoot Morgan first, Deal and Dixie Lee posed the greatest danger to Felicia. He had to prevent them from entering the gorge.

It was Jessica Tandy who gazed into the gorge, then cried out, "Look! There! It's the schoolmarm!"

"She's seen us!" Dixie cried, vaulting into the saddle. He spurred his mount and raced ahead of Tandy and Pony Deal. Leveling his rifle, he shouted, "She's mine! All mine!"

Fargo had other ideas. His finger curled around the trigger; the Sharps boomed and bucked. The heavy slug slammed into Dixie Lee's chest, hurling him from his horse. Fargo didn't wait to see the short killer fall. Pivoting toward Pony Deal, he levered the trigger guard of the Sharps and fed in another cartridge.

The gunman was incredibly fast. The instant the Sharps thundered, Pony Deal shifted, clearing leather in a blur. He fanned his pistol three times, the shots ricocheting off the boulder within inches of where Fargo stood.

Fargo trained the Sharps a second time. Deal was already launching himself into the air, but he was a shade too slow. Fargo put a slug into the gambler's fancy white shirt, right above the heart.

Frederick Morgan and Jessica Tandy were also in motion. Morgan dived into the high grass. The woman produced a revolver and fired twice at the boulder. To Fargo's surprise, she was an excellent shot. The bullets sent rock chips flying into his face. He stepped back, inserted another cartridge, and crouched.

Jessica and Morgan had disappeared. The four horses were milling in confusion, making it hard for Fargo to spot movement beyond the fire. He sidled out from behind the boulder and over to a smaller one. Resting the Sharps on top, he waited for one of them to show themselves.

For a while all was still. Then Fargo glimpsed a vague shape retreating toward the pines. He led the figure by a few steps, held his breath, and when the person filled his sights, he fired.

None other than Frederick Morgan shot erect, his mouth wide but no sound coming out, his hand pressed to a spurting wound in his side. Morgan twisted toward Fargo, tried to raise his pistol, then collapsed, landing in the open on his stomach. He was severely wounded but far from dead. Fargo saw his attempt to lift his gun arm.

Tandy was stealthier than her boss. Fargo looked and looked but saw no sign of her. Figuring that she must be lying low somewhere nearby, he bent at the waist and darted back to the huge boulder. He expected to draw her fire, but he reached safety without a single shot ringing out.

Fargo checked on Morgan and saw the man had propped himself up on his elbows. Fargo quickly backed up, his intent being to circle around and sneak up on Morgan from behind.

But he had hardly taken three steps when the barrel of a pistol was jammed into the base of his skull.

"Surprise, surprise, you handsome son of a bitch."

Jessica Tandy's voice was as cold as ice. Fargo made no sudden moves, his every nerve on edge, painfully aware that all she had to do was squeeze the trigger and he was dead.

"Drop the rifle and put your hands over your head," Tandy commanded.

Fargo had to comply. She shoved him into the open and stepped around to the left to better cover him.

"Look what I found, Fred. Do you want the honors or should I do it?"

Morgan was on one knee. Red spittle flecked his lips as he grinned and slowly elevated his revolver. "Let me," he croaked. "He's all mine."

From out of nowhere came the pounding of hooves. Fargo saw Morgan glance past him, saw Jessica begin to whirl. He threw himself to the side, drawing as he moved, and although Morgan snapped off a shot, it missed. As his own revolver blasted twice, he heard a horse whinny, heard Jessica Tandy scream and the crunch of breaking bones.

Just like that, it was finally over. Frederick Morgan lay on his back, his nose sporting a new set of nostrils. Jessica Tandy lay in a twisted heap, her body resembling a broken rag doll.

Felicia, calming her prancing horse, stared in horror. "I didn't mean to run her down like that," she said, aghast. "I only wanted to keep her from shooting you."

Lowering the pistol, Fargo stepped over to her mount. "You didn't do as I wanted."

"No, I didn't," Felicia admitted, a contagious grin tugging at her mouth. "I just couldn't bear the thought of you being harmed." She slid off, into his open arms. "I hope you won't hold it against me."

"I have half a mind to put you over my knee and paddle you," Fargo joked.

"Would you?" the schoolmarm asked, and pressed herself against him.

LOOKING FORWARD!
The following is the opening
section from the next novel in the exciting
Trailsman series from Signet:

THE TRAILSMAN #167
BLACK MESA TREACHERY

The high plateau near Santa Fe, 1860,
A harsh land of red rock and rolling thunder
where some men find the face of God
and others do the Devil's work . . .

"You Skye Fargo?"

The tall man with the lake blue eyes glanced up from his whiskey at the rotund bartender who had spoken. Another man standing nearby, foot hooked over the bar rail and beer in hand, nudged his companion and the two of them gawked at the tall stranger.

"Did you hear that? That's Skye Fargo," one of them whispered to the other. "They call him the Trailsman. I heard all about him."

"Yeah, me too," the other whispered back, awe in his voice. "Wonder what he's doing down here in Taos?"

Skye Fargo nodded once to the bartender, paying no attention to the two men.

"Forgot to tell you earlier when you came in, Mister Fargo. Got a message for you," the bartender said, handing him a folded paper.

Fargo took it and pushed his empty glass across the bar and shook his head, refusing a refill. He examined the writing on the front envelope—his name in bold black letters— and the large wax seal on the back with its crucifix, initialed A and F. Yeah, it was the message he'd been waiting for all afternoon. He glared at the bartender, suspecting him of holding the letter back in order to sell a few more drinks. As he broke the seal, Fargo gazed around the half-deserted bar. Late afternoon sun poured in past the batwing doors. In a dark corner four men were playing a dead earnest game of poker as they had been all afternoon. A dove in a faded green dress was talking to a heavyset fellow, a rancher by the looks of him. And then there were the two men—cowpoke types—standing next to him and staring at his every move. Fargo turned away from them and opened the paper.

Meet him at Castle Rock on the Thunder Trail, edge of Tewa land. At moonrise. Bring him to Chimayò. Meanwhile, travel incognito—danger everywhere. Go with God. Amado Fernandez

Moonrise. That was around midnight. Fargo glanced at the golden light across the warped board floor. It was getting on sunset. He'd never make it in time. It was at least five or six hours of fast riding to the rendezvous point. Hastily, he pulled a couple of coins out of his pocket, threw them on the counter, and turned to go.

"Hey! Hey!" one of the cowpokes called after him as he headed toward the door. "Ain't you Skye Fargo? Ain't you the Trailsman?" The men at the poker table lowered their cards and craned their necks to stare at him. Then a couple of them pointed at him and muttered to one another. Fargo ignored them all and pushed through the doors. Great. Everybody in the Taos barroom had got a good look at him. And the message had said to travel incognito. Well, at least he'd be out of town in no time.

At the stable he asked for the Ovaro and the stable boy brought it out. The pinto's black-and-white coat gleamed magnificently in the slanting light. It nuzzled Fargo.

"Beautiful horse you got here, Mister Fargo," the boy said, stroking the pinto's neck, reluctant to let go of the reins. Fargo mounted. The pinto moved restlessly under him, eager to be away on the trail.

"You're awful popular, Mister Fargo," the boy said.

"What do you mean?"

"Those two guys looking for you," the kid said. "I told them you were over at the hotel. Didn't they find you?"

"Two guys? What did they look like?"

The boy screwed up his face, remembering.

"The first was one of them Catholic padres. Came in on a donkey around midday. Said he had some letter for you." Fargo nodded, saying nothing. Yes, the brother who had brought the message from Padre Amado Fernandez. "And then just a quarter hour ago. Big fellow. Tall and all dressed in black. Smart like. Riding a chestnut. I asked if he didn't want to stable her, but he said he was in a hurry to find you. Was in an awful bad mood."

Fargo sat for a moment, in thought. Who was the man in black who'd followed him to Taos? Sounded like trouble for sure. Meanwhile, the sun was dropping swiftly over the distant mountain, staining the clouds bloodred. There was no time to lose, no time to find out what trouble was after him now. He had a job to do, a promise to keep. Fargo pulled a coin out of his pocket and flipped it to the kid.

"Tell him you found out I was heading due north. Up to Ute Country."

"Sure. Sure, Mister Fargo."

Fargo headed out, riding through the back streets toward the head of the trail that led south out of Taos. But the question preyed on his mind. Who the hell was on his tail? He decided to have a quick look and turned back into the alley that led toward the main square. He dismounted and walked forward to stand at the corner of a storefront where he was out of sight but had a good view.

All around the square bars were just starting to heat up for the night. The strains of a honky-tonk piano floated on the air, and several knots of men came into sight, swaggering in different directions toward the various watering holes. A line of horses was hitched in front of the Taos Hotel. Among them stood a glistening black-pointed chestnut. As Fargo watched, a tall broad-shouldered man dressed all in black came out of the front door of the hotel. Even from a distance, Fargo's keen gaze could discern his broken nose and his glittering black eyes. Fargo searched his mind, but couldn't remember having seen the face before. The tall man paused for a moment, looked up and down the square, and then stepped down the stairs, heading for one of the bars. Just then, Fargo spotted the stable boy running up the dusty street in pursuit to tell the stranger that he had headed north. Fargo didn't wait, but turned back, mounted the pinto and galloped out of town.

Who the hell was the big man? He'd never seen him before, but he could have been sent by any one of a hundred men who had reason to hunt him down, thought Fargo. If the man lived hard and fast, he made a lot of friends and just about as many enemies. Anyway, the kid would throw the stranger off his scent. There was no time to deal with him now.

The pinto's powerful legs pounded the trail as they climbed the hill. Soon the town of Taos lay behind them, a clutter of board and adobe buildings at the foot of the high snowy peaks to the east. West of town the sage plain stretched for miles toward the mountains at the horizon. As he gained the crest of the hill and the flatland fell away below, Fargo spotted the dark jagged line of the gorge where the mighty Rio Grande cut deep into the earth.

But right now his business lay to the south, and as they came over the top of the hill, Taos and the gorge disappeared from view and Fargo's thoughts turned to what lay ahead. It had been a few weeks since the first message had come from Padre Amado Fernandez. Fargo had met the priest years before at a mission in California. Fernandez had struck him as one of the few holy men who seemed to have his feet on the ground. In his California parish the priest had built an orphanage and a hospital and then got the whole town reorganized after it had been burnt to the ground by a raging brush fire. He'd had one of the most successful missions in the whole country. Then the local archbishop transferred him down to the famous Chimayò Mission near Santa Fe. That had been five years ago, and Fargo hadn't heard a word about Amado Fernandez since.

Then, the week before, a letter found him up in Kansas. The padre wrote that he needed Fargo's help. The instructions were to go to Taos and wait at the bar for a message. Fargo wondered what kind of trouble the padre could have got himself into. The message had said meet "him." But who was he supposed to be meeting at Castle Rock? Well, he'd find out soon enough.

The sunset colors were fading in the west and ahead of

him the first star appeared over the southern horizon which was sharp with buttes. The trail arched over the hills, curved through the dense and fragrant piñons, then descended toward the rocky, open land.

He road hard toward the rendezvous point—Thunder Trail and Castle Rock near Black Mesa. Fargo knew the mesa, a mammoth hulk of rock and earth with sheer cliffs rising straight up from the flat land below. Black Mesa could be seen for hundreds of miles around. But no matter how sunny the day, Black Mesa always seemed to be in shadow and now, with the light fading steadily, it was a darker shadow in the shade of the mountains to the west. He headed toward the spot, the pinto galloping full out on the hard-packed trail. No time to lose. It was a good five hours' ride to Castle Rock. And by then the moon would be up. He was going to be late. Whoever he was supposed to be meeting there would just have to wait.

The moon was a bright silver coin high in the black heavens. Fargo stood and stretched his limbs, then leaned against the night-cold stone in the shadow of Castle Rock. All around him the nubby sage was like a woolen blanket folded over the moon-washed hills. A few miles away, the huge dark shape of Black Mesa blocked out the stars in the sky. Fargo listened to the coyotes singing and the whir of bats and owls as they hunted. No one had come. He'd arrived about an hour after moonrise and had been waiting a good two hours more.

Fargo pulled up the collar of his buckskin jacket as the desert wind turned colder. Whoever it was had either given up on him before he'd arrived or wasn't going to show. He was just beginning to wonder if he ought to ride on to Chimayò, when he saw it.

Movement. In the brush at the top of the hill. The Ovaro, hidden in the shadow of the rock, pawed nervously. Its keen nostrils had picked up the scent of something.

Yes, movement above on the hill. A figure walking in the brush. Then two, three. Fargo slid the Colt from its holster and the moonlight gleamed blue on the barrel. There was a long, wavering line of dark figures walking through sage, spread out across the hill as if searching, their heads bent low. As they came nearer, Fargo saw that they were all robed and hooded. Monks. He felt relief wash over him. He holstered his pistol and walked out to meet them.

His boots crunched on the gravel trail, and the line came to a halt. Fargo raised a hand in greeting as he neared.

"What are you looking for?" he called out.

There was a long silence, and then one of the monks stepped forward, his face hidden in the shadow beneath his cowl.

"Who are you?" the monk said gruffly.

Fargo suddenly felt a sensation of danger. Something was wrong. He must be on his guard his instincts told him. Fargo didn't hesitate a second.

"Name's Brent Barker, Father," Fargo said in a loud and friendly voice. He kept his head down under his low hat brim, his face hidden from the glare of moonlight. "Heading down to Santa Fe. I think I took a wrong turn. I'd be much obliged if you could tell me which way it is."

The monks stood in silence for a long moment. Then the rough voice answered him again.

"Turn around, stranger," the monk said. "Santa Fe's over that way. About fifteen miles." He pointed across the broken land toward the southeast.

"Thank you kindly," Fargo said, backing away. "Since it's so late, I guess I'll just camp here for the night and head out there in the morning." Maybe, he thought, whoever was supposed to meet him might still be coming.

"This is Tewa land," the monk said, his thick voice hard-edged. "And we've had some trouble out here. We don't like trespassers."

"Really?" Fargo said, keeping up the ruse of naivete. "I heard of the Tewa tribe. Now, are *you* Tewa?"

"This is Tewa land," the monk repeated sternly. Fargo saw the glint of a rifle emerge from the folds of the dark robe. "And we are from the Tewa Mission."

"I guess so," Fargo said. He returned to the shadow of Castle Rock and mounted the Ovaro. As he rode off, he turned and looked back. The dark figures of the monks were ranged across the hillside. They stood, silent and still, watching him ride off. Who ever heard of a monk toting a rifle? He wondered what connection they had with the stranger he was supposed to have met at Castle Rock. Maybe he could get that question answered by Padre Amado Fernandez at Chimayò.

He had gone scarcely a mile and was just galloping up out of a shallow arroyo when the Ovaro shied and nickered. Fargo knew the signal. The pinto sensed something out there in the darkness—something that didn't belong. Fargo reined in and sat for a long moment, looking about him, his senses alert. The pinto moved nervously under him. Then he heard a sound, so faint another man would have missed it.

Fargo dismounted, drew his Colt, and made his way through the brush and pale summer-dry grass. He heard the sound again. Unmistakable. A human noise, a moan. An instant later, he glimpsed a dark form—a man. Fargo glanced around, then bent over and turned him face up.

He was wearing a monk's robe. The moonlight fell

across his face, which was badly disfigured. The nose had been smashed and the cheeks cut deep. Blood blackened his features so that Fargo could barely distinguish his features. The man tried to open his eyes and finally managed it. His lips parted, blood ran from his mouth, and Fargo heard the terrible moan again. Then he realized the man's tongue had been cut out.

"Take it easy," Fargo said, wondering if this was the man he was supposed to meet. He propped him against a rock. He didn't have long to live. That was for certain and there was nothing Fargo could do for him. Not even a drink of water would ease his suffering now.

"Who did this to you?" Fargo asked.

The man moaned and moved his head from side to side. Fargo felt his frustration. How could he communicate?

"I came to Castle Rock tonight to meet somebody," Fargo tried again. "Padre Amado Fernandez sent me."

At the padre's name, the man's eyes fluttered again and then fixed on Fargo's face with a look of sudden hope, terrible in its desperation. His hand stirred against Fargo and he moaned. Fargo felt the man trying to press something into his hand, and Fargo took it, then held it out into the moonlight. It was a length of rope, knotted rope.

"Is this a message?" Fargo asked. "For Amado Fernandez?" The dying man nodded slowly. His breath was strained now, rasping, and he brought his hands together, working. Fargo saw that he was trying to get his ring off his finger. Fargo removed the ring. Then the man's hand scrabbled at the soil and came up with a handful of it, pressing it into Fargo's hand. He breathed once, heavily, and then no more.

Fargo felt the dry earth trickling through his fingers as he looked down at the dead man. The pinto nickered, almost silently. He glanced up to see the line of monks descending the slope. Swiftly, Fargo melted into the shadow of the nearby cutbank and pulled the Ovaro with him into the cover of thick brush. A few minutes later, he heard the sounds of the approaching men.

"Over here!" one shouted. Fargo peered out from the brush and saw the dark shapes of the robed monks gathering around the dead man. Maybe he could find out what this was all about. But they did not speak. They hoisted the corpse on their shoulders and then moved off. Fargo watched as the silent procession disappeared over the hill.

Fargo wondered at the strange monk with the rifle who had warned him off the Tewa land. The monks had been searching for the one who'd been tortured. To rescue him? Or to kill him?